CHRISTMAS COMFORT

SOUL SISTERS AT CEDAR MOUNTAIN LODGE, BOOK 17

EV BISHOP

For my huge, diverse family—especially my lovely stepmom and my sisters, Laura, *Jo, and Ellie.
That's not a typo. Just like Stevie, I also have a treasured sister named Jo. That's where our similarities end, though!

ALSO BY EV BISHOP

SOUL SISTERS AT CEDAR MOUNTAIN LODGE

Creamy vanilla, a kiss of ginger, melting chocolate . . . The aroma of baking Christmas cookies wafted through the house, mingling with the rich, earthy scent of freshly brewed coffee. The cozy smell should've made Stevie feel warm-hearted and misty-eyed with gratitude and excitement about the upcoming holiday season. Instead, she felt the exact opposite, and the tears prickling the back of her eyes and aching in her throat were dread, not anticipation. Her jaw was tight with anger, and her hands were clenched into fists as she glared at her reflection in the big bathroom mirror.

"Snap out of it, Fox," she hissed. "You're being ridiculous. Focus on the good!"

It was excellent advice. She had so, so much to be thankful for, after all. And she knew it. She did. Was still astonished at her good fortune, actually. That all this was hers: The roomy yet cozy three-bedroom home, so sunshiny and welcoming with its abundance of windows, butter yellow walls, and natural wood accents. The chef's dream of a kitchen, all marble, stainless steel, and African hardwood.

1

Their successful pub, Fox & Hound. And, more importantly —in fact, the only things of real importance—her family. Jackson, her husband of almost six years, her precious little son Joe, named after his Auntie Jo, Stevie's sister and best friend, and her family—by adoption *and* soul connection, including her mother Maddie, and sisters Jo, Alissa, and Hailey.

Even her relationship with her birth mother, Marilyn, was healing, something Stevie had dreamed of since she was a little girl but for a long time had almost given up on. And then, miracle of miracles, Marilyn had finally gotten sober and stayed that way.

Stevie jabbed at her eyelashes with her mascara wand, gave her mouth a vicious swipe of lip gloss, and sprayed her hair one more time, willing her unruly carrot red mop to stay contained in its sleek, low ponytail. She gave herself another critical once over, then tried a tentative smile. She was almost, *almost*, satisfied. She looked like her sister Jo, style-wise anyway. That meant she'd fit in with the other moms, looks-wise, at least.

Mentally reviewing her day's to-do list for the umpteenth time, Stevie stepped back from the mirror just as the bathroom door flew open. She collided with a very masculine—and very familiar—chest. Jackson. The impact caused her to stumble a bit.

"Mmm," he said, smiling as he caught her and kept her from falling. "It's been a while since you threw yourself at me. I like it."

Stevie wanted nothing more than to sink into him and revel in the new citrusy cologne he'd started wearing, but she didn't have time.

As his arms went around her and he started to pull her close, she reared back. "Don't! You'll mess up my hair."

Her voice was sharper than she'd intended. Jackson

dropped his arms and stepped away like she'd slapped him. And she got it. Words could be like that.

"I'll *mess up your hair*? Are you kidding me?" He rolled his eyes, but there was no good-humored ribbing in it. The sudden flint in his expression and the granite in his jaw made Stevie's heart hurt.

"Jackson . . . " she whispered, half plea, half prayer, but she was talking to his back. He'd already retreated through the door he'd so recently appeared in.

She moved to follow him.

"Jackson—" she said again, and he half turned as if he might come back toward her. Then the insistent buzz of his phone interrupted. He held up a hand to Stevie as if to communicate, *Whatever you're about to say, don't bother.* Then his full focus was on the device pulled from his pocket.

Stevie hated herself for despising the smile that suddenly erased Jackson's grim expression. But she knew full well who had texted him this early in the morning. The same somebody who always seemed to be texting him these days.

She has good reason to, she reminded herself. *She does.*

Uh huh, whispered a different insidious inner voice. *Uh huh.*

CHAPTER 2

Swallowing back her unhappiness about the botched moment—yet again, it seemed—with Jackson, Stevie did allow herself a minute she didn't have to snuggle Joey. She scooped him up from the loveseat in their living room, where he was bundled up with Syd, their grizzled little terrier buddy, under a fuzzy gray blanket. Both boy and dog seemed equally absorbed in Joey's favorite TV show, *Cookie Monster's Foodie Truck*. The old saying that the apple didn't fall far from the tree proved true with her and Jackson's offspring, for sure. Joey was already just as interested in all things yummy as they were. Physically, too, he was the spitting image of his daddy, with Jackson's dark curls and huge brown eyes.

"Hey!" Joey said as she clicked off the TV, but his mild objection turned into a giggle as Stevie tickled his neck by pretending to munch on him.

"Mmm, cookies!" she rumbled in her best impersonation of the google-eyed blue monster and nibbled Joey's neck again. "Me *love* cookies!"

"But I'm not a cookie," he shrieked with glee. "I'm not!"

They were both laughing as she got him dressed for the outdoors in a heavy coat, soft fleece cap with ear flaps, waterproof mittens, and ultra-warm boots. She had contemplated snow pants, but his little pull-on sports pants were made by a small company in British Columbia, Canada, and were fleece-lined and water-repellant. Plus, it was a mild day by Granite Ridge's winter standards. Stevie already knew she was in danger of being a helicopter mom. She didn't want to boil her son to death on top of everything else.

Joey was so cute bundled up like a little woodsman that Stevie's breath caught. And he'd never been cold or worn clothes unsuitable for the weather, something other people might take for granted but that she was always consciously grateful about.

"Are you excited, little man?" she asked.

"Yes!" He cheered. "We're going on a Christmas tree hunt, going to catch us a Christmas tree!"

Stevie grinned at his copycatting of his Auntie Jo's play on the old children's story about going on a lion hunt. Jo made the same silly, fun joke every year as she planned the tree-getting excursion. Stevie's eyes misted. At just five years old, Joey already had Christmas traditions with his family—and what a family. So many people who loved him, including his cousins Ollie and Grace, who doted on him like he was a precious younger sibling. As awed and thankful as Stevie was for everything Joey got to enjoy, part of her felt . . . pressured. What if she couldn't sustain this beautiful, charmed life for her little boy? All parents wanted the best for their children, but how many could actually pull it off? Her brain flashed on Jackson's facial expression when he got that recent text, and her insides went cold with a feeling of foreboding that she recognized all too well from her own childhood.

Exactly. You can't keep this. It's all a dream. It's too good to be true, and deep down, you know it.

Stevie wanted to pooh-pooh the negative thought, but that was the thing lately, wasn't it? She knew or feared—based on life experiences and hard-won insight—that the awful voice was probably right.

Her grim thoughts were interrupted by the rumble of a large engine in the driveway. Saved by Jo! Stevie opened the door before her sister had a chance to ring the doorbell.

"Auntie Jo! Auntie Jo!" Joey cheered, lifting his arms to his treasured aunt. One day soon, Joey would be too big for Jo to lift and let him wrap himself monkey-like around her, but today was not that day.

Looking like she'd just stepped out of a magazine for outdoor living in her tall leather boots, smart wool jacket, and matching scarf and beanie, Jo plucked her nephew up and gave him a noisy kiss. Stevie's heart swelled as it always did to see Jo's love for Joey. That, at the very least, was something Stevie could always count on.

"Are you ready for Christmas tree hunting, my man?" Jo asked Joey. He chirped back in excitement, but Stevie, still distracted, didn't catch exactly what he said. She did notice, however, a look of concern in Jo's warm eyes and furrowed brow.

"Sorry, I'm late," Jo said. "The kids, you know . . ." Her voice trailed off in apology. Stevie waved her hand to brush it away. Despite her worries about her day's to-do list, she hadn't even noticed Jo was late. Jo's concern didn't appear soothed. She peered at Stevie intently. "Are you okay?"

The question gave Stevie pause. Did Jo see that Stevie wasn't coping the way she and her other sisters were? Was it obvious to those who loved her best that she wasn't as good at marriage and, well, everything, as they were? She really didn't have time to ask though—and, also, the last thing she wanted was for her busy, competent, amazing sister to have to worry about her.

"Yeah, fine. Just busy."

Jo didn't seem super convinced, but Ollie and Grace had rolled down their windows and were calling Joey excitedly.

Stevie blew kisses to her adorable niece and nephew and waved at Jo's sister-in-law Gina, who was riding shotgun. How Stevie wished she could just bail on her responsibilities for the day and go with them. A pang of wistfulness made her stomach clench, and she frowned—then caught her expression mirrored on Jo's face.

Jo didn't question her further, though. Just firmed up details about the day's outing and refused Steve's offer to pay for the tree, insisting it was their treat.

Stevie thanked her sister, gave Joey a big hug, and told him to have fun, then slipped back inside and shut the door so her gloomy expression wouldn't sour their day.

"Snap out of it, Fox!" she commanded herself for the second time that day, and, also for the second time that day, she knew whatever she was going through would take more than a one-line command to fix. But first things first. She had baking to box up and deliver.

CHAPTER 3

Stevie fastened Syd into his seat-belted basket in the van's front passenger seat, backed carefully out of the driveway, then frowned at herself in the rear-view mirror before pulling in behind a BMW SUV heading toward town from her little residential cul-de-sac. She should be going over a mental list of everything she needed to get done before Jo returned with Joey and a Christmas tree that would need trimming. Instead, she found herself obsessing—again—about Jackson. He'd left the house after their bathroom run-in that morning without a note or saying goodbye. She'd heard him talking to Joey and telling him to have a good day but didn't check in as to who was picking him up later. Did he even know there was no kindergarten today and that he was with his aunt? Stevie couldn't remember if she'd gotten a chance to tell him.

No doubt, Jackson had just gone to Fox & Hound, and she'd see him shortly, but it was inconsiderate. Or was it? She wasn't always sure. Maybe her expectations were too high? Or too low? She'd never had two parents, and Marilyn had been undependable, to say the least. Even in primary school,

Stevie had never counted on Marilyn arriving to walk her home—not even during times when they'd moved yet again and the apartment's address wasn't fully locked into Stevie's memory. And Maddie was a role model mother—but again, had been single while taking care of her, Jo, Alissa, and Hailey. How did two-parent families coordinate things? She'd tried to discuss it with Jackson, along with so many other things, so many times, but he always shut the conversation down or shrugged her concerns off. When and why had he stopped talking with her?

Traffic picked up as Stevie got closer to downtown, but that didn't bother her. She was always careful when she drove—precious cargo and all that—and the roads were miraculously clear and well plowed for this time of year, the sky was clear, and visibility was great. She let out a sigh that didn't fit the beauty of the morning and forced her mind off her husband and her bazillion insecurities and onto all the things she had to get done today.

Call Marilyn about stall set-up for the Season of Giving fundraiser at Cedar Mountain Lodge's Winterfest and confirm the soups Marilyn, Jamie, and John wanted her to make.

Selling soup, both hot and ready-to-eat while wandering about the festival and premade mixes for people to store in their pantries or give as gifts, was the perfect fundraiser for the Pioneer Street Soup kitchen, and Stevie smiled despite her mood. The big fundraiser, featuring booths and stalls of a huge variety, all raising money for causes near and dear to Granite Ridgeans' hearts, was one part of the hectic lead-up to Christmas she was genuinely looking forward to. And she couldn't wait to make a wreath—or wreaths!—with Joey and Jackson at the booth that Jo was organizing to raise funds for her foster organization, Love Links.

Maddie and her sister Lindsey's booth would be selling

cute leashes and collars made by high school volunteers to raise money for their new charity, Sunset Paws Pet Hospice, and offering low-cost vaccines onsite as a community service. They'd even have dogs and cats at the booth available for adoption—though potential pet parents would need to be screened first, so no pets would be going home that day. All in all, it would be fabulous fun, though Syd, who'd be in doggy daycare up at the lodge for most of it, might not see it quite the same way.

As if reading her mind, Syd grumbled in his sleep from his cushion on the passenger seat. Stevie smiled over at her little black and tan bristle brush of a companion of six years, then gave his silky black ears—the softest part on him—an affectionate rub. The Terrier X had been a Christmas present from Jackson when they reconnected as adults, years after their disastrous high school love affair.

But back on the Season of Giving note—right! Thank goodness, she'd remembered. The last meeting for the fundraiser committee was tonight at Granite Grind. Marilyn had the art therapy class she led tonight, and Stevie had promised to attend on her behalf to hear all the set-up rules and last-minute details. She sighed, and her mind raced on. That meeting was at seven. She had two days of work to fit in before then, including . . .

Brainstorm and confirm the pub's Christmas through New Year's specials. Then place the grocery and booze orders early so if any restaurant in town got shorted, it wasn't the Fox & Hound.

Interview for a new sous chef and a prep cook. Really, they needed another dishwasher too, but at least the young woman they'd recently hired seemed like she'd be reliable.

Approve the renovation plans—finally gotten right—for the vacant steakhouse soon to be Fox & Hound II, aka "Two," their new pub set to open in just three months in the nearby community of Dawson. Pay the contractor's first installment. Stevie's stomach clenched into a hard fist, and as she stopped at a red light, she forced herself to take a deep breath. Inhale for seven seconds. Hold for seven seconds. Release—

The light turned green. Thankfully, her thoughts moved on as the traffic did.

Drop off cookies at Joe's school, "Greenridge Young Learners Academy"—such a pretentious thing to call a kindergarten, she thought—by . . . Stevie checked her phone for the time and yelped. Ten minutes from now.

She'd planned to pop by the pub first, but that would have to wait.

The *Academy*—Stevie always gave it italics in her mind—was buzzing with parents. Rats. She'd been hoping to slip in, see only the teacher, and drop off her goodies, which could be frozen until they needed them for their own Season of Giving booth at Cedar Mountain Lodge. No. Such. Luck. Apparently, everyone was in the same boat as her, dropping off before heading to work. Or to whatever it was that rich people did all day. Come to think of it, she recognized several of the "parents" as nannies. A trickle of relief melted some of her anxiety. She always fit in better with staff than with the moms and dads. At the beginning of the year "gala" event—another fundraiser, which struck Stevie as crazy because the kids all paid exorbitant tuition—she'd come straight from work. In her all-black—and she thought quite lovely—professional attire, she'd been mistaken for a server. She'd thought it was hilarious, until she saw Jackson's reaction. He'd been incensed, embarrassed almost, or something. Was that the kick-off to this newest batch of insecurities that always seemed on high boil inside her these days? Whether it was or wasn't, she'd gotten Jo to take her shopping. She obviously needed a different wardrobe for this new life of hers.

She climbed out of her van, and Syd lifted his head and raised an inquisitive ear.

"I'll be right back. I promise," she said, collecting the heavy tote of carefully packaged assorted cookies.

Syd sighed agreeably and went back to snoozing.

"Stevie!" The shriek—and it was a shriek: a blood-curdling *Steeeeveeee* in a too-gleeful, too-high soprano to be genuine. Stevie felt her face burn as she realized she'd visibly flinched. She tightened her grip on her tote's handles.

"Your pantsuit is just sooooo cute!" Again the words were screeched at a decibel pitch that could cause ear bleeding. Several heads turned. Stevie wished she'd just said fudge it— the full strength of her potty mouth these days, thanks to Joey—and worn her chef blacks.

"It must be a blah-blah-blah."

Stevie looked down at her clothing, feeling a flush of pleasure despite herself. She'd gotten her clothes right finally. Maybe Jackson was right. If she'd just give the other moms here a chance and not be so prickly, maybe they could be friendly at least, if not true friends.

"Thanks," Stevie said, hating that she, of all people, sounded shy. Who was she these days?

"I mean, it's obviously last season's blah-blah-blah, but that's all right. It's still . . . so cute."

The woman—Farrah, her brain threw the name, and Stevie grabbed it with relief—hadn't actually said "blah, blah, blah," of course. For the life of her, though, Stevie couldn't hold on to designer clothing brand names. Not even for a second. If you wanted to discuss the best cheeses to eat with you-name-it, talk about easy but sumptuous appetizers for any occasion, or discover how to get tomato-based stains out of your favorite gray hoodie? Then she was your woman. Stevie knew Farrah did not want to discuss those types of things, however. She squeezed her eyes shut, reminded herself that everyone eats, so everyone had something in common, put a smile on her face, and turned around.

"Farrah, *hi*. Great to see you—and yeah, last season. You got me. Always a bit behind the times. How are you?" See, she could do social niceties. She made a note to tell Jo, who would definitely laugh and not quite believe her.

Farrah's head swiveled on her long, swanlike neck. Why was "swanlike" a description that seemed to fit rich folks so well? She was wearing skinny jeans that looked painted on and a bomber jacket with a fur-lined hood that even Stevie could tell was definitely a blah-blah-blah of some kind or another. Her heavily lashed blue eyes scanned the distance between Stevie and her white van with its very discernible Fox & Hound decals. "And where's that yummy husband of yours?" she crooned.

And then again, every establishment reserved the right to refuse service. Stevie let her smile drop. She preferred to only give genuine ones anyway. "He's having hemorrhoid surgery."

Farrah's eyes widened. "Ohhhh, noooo, I hope he'll be okay?"

"Oh, he'll be fine," Stevie assured Farrah. "You know what they say about hemorrhoids."

"Um, no . . ."

"They're a pain in the butt, but they're not life-threatening."

Farrah's plump lips pursed in distaste, and she looked through Stevie. Then her hand flew up as if to wave at someone in the distance and catch their attention.

Stevie's farewell smile was authentic. "Have a great Christmas, Farrah," she called as Farrah tottered away on her high-heeled winter boots.

"I think we both know who the real pain in the butt is here." Ana, Joey's friend Zachary's nanny, fell into stride beside Stevie, carrying a stack of five pie boxes tied with gingham ribbons. "I do hope Mr. Bassett mends quickly, though."

Stevie laughed and cringed with a smidge of shame, but only a really, really tiny one. "*Jackson*. Mr. Bassett's his dad. And Jackson's not really having surgery—and he doesn't have hemorrhoids. I just want Farrah to have that mental picture every time she inappropriately ogles my husband."

Ana's laugh was soft, but her dark eyes shone with sharp mirth. "You're evil!"

"See? *You* get me!"

Ana chuckled again. "You really shouldn't mind the moms daydreaming about your husband, though. Most of them are married to old grandfather men."

That was true—and though Stevie berated herself inwardly for being judgemental in this way, she just didn't get it. So many young women who seemed content to be a second—or third—wife for some midlife crisis creep twenty or even thirty years older than them. Several kids in Joey's class were second families and had older siblings almost as old as Stevie. Or the moms were fifteen years older than her, power women in their own careers, who had their first—or multiple children in quick succession—in their forties when their biological clocks sounded final alarms. Stevie was both inspired and intimidated by how those moms seemed to rule every domain they came into contact with. They were also not only more interesting than the Farrah-types, they were generally kinder, but so busy anything like real friendship was ruled out. And fair enough.

"It's the wallets," Ana said knowingly, but then, as if sensing Stevie was uncomfortable with the direction of the conversation, she changed subjects. "Tell me what you brought. I made empanadas. Twelve in a box. They're already frozen but reheat really nicely."

Always more a salty than sweet personality—surprise, surprise!—empanadas were far more exciting to Stevie than pies would've been, and she and Ana happily chatted about food as they dropped off their donations.

Taking their time in the hallway, admiring the kids' cute Christmas artwork that decorated the walls, Ana bumped into someone else she knew—a woman somewhere near Stevie's age, so mid-thirties or so, with an angular black bob, olive skin, and striking blue eyes. Ana introduced her to Stevie as Inez, the nanny of twins in the classroom across the hall from Joey and Zachary.

Inez joined them as they made their way out of the school and across the parking lot. As they chatted, it turned out that Inez's sister Callie was a new dishwasher at Fox & Hound.

"It's really hard work," Stevie said.

"Yes, but she's hoping they'll let her move up. She loves to cook."

"I had no idea! She should've said when she applied. I have a prep cook position open."

Inez stopped walking, and her mouth fell open slightly.

"What?" Stevie asked, slightly alarmed. How had she blundered now? Usually food-related anything was safe ground.

"*You* have a prep cook position open?"

"Yes . . ." Stevie didn't understand the emphasis on "you."

Ana's eyes widened, and she sucked her lips in, making her mouth a cartoonish-straight line. Obviously, *she* knew what the problem was.

"Stevie doesn't just work at the Fox & Hound. She's Stevie *Fox Bassett*. She is the fox in Fox & Hound," she said carefully.

Inez still looked confused—and then awareness sparked in her blue eyes.

"You mean you own the pub? You are the owner."

Stevie shrugged uncomfortably. It still blew her away too. "Guilty as charged. Well, me and my husband, anyway."

"But you are a dishwasher. Callie says you work very hard and clean the kitchen very thoroughly. She worked with you last shift. I thought you were a nanny like us and washed dishes at night. Two jobs."

Stevie grinned. "Only one job officially, but it feels like ten sometimes. We were short. I do whatever is needed, plus I'm a control freak. I like to train all positions.

Inez finally returned Stevie's smile. "I'm impressed—but no, about control. My sister says you are 'awesome.'"

Stevie winked. "Well, remember, I do pay her."

Inez's smile deepened and she shook her head.

"Miss Stevie is different than some here," Ana said, gesturing toward the school. Stevie noticed her slip back to referring to her as Miss Stevie the way she used to when they first met, but she didn't comment on it for now.

"So why do you have your son in this school?" Inez asked.

"Because it will pave the way for him," Ana said matter-of-factly. "And this is where he belongs. He's from a rich family."

Stevie shook her head, unhappy that Ana had answered for her and gotten it all wrong, though her answer wasn't much better. "He's just a little boy. I want him to have a nice childhood. That's all for now. Money is convenient and necessary to a point, but it's not my top value. Nowhere close."

Ana and Inez looked skeptical. Stevie didn't blame them. Her attitude about money was very privileged, and she knew it. It was so weird to be one of the has'es. When she was a little girl, her most consistent fantasy was winning the lottery. She'd thought "being rich" would fix Marilyn and everything else in her life, too. It was easy to say money didn't matter or wasn't the most important thing when you had enough of it that you didn't worry every single month if you'd be able to cover rent and keep the heat on.

"It means a lot to Joey's dad that he attends here," Stevie added.

Joey's dad. That she had referred to Jackson that way made a shiver go down Stevie's back. When had the love of her life become merely "Joey's dad," and when had his goal for his son become so divergent from hers?

As Stevie hit the unlock button on her key fob for the van, Farrah, accompanied by Morgan and Monica, two other moms of kids in Joey's class, appeared by Farrah's Lexus, which was parked nearby.

"Hiiii again," Farrah chirped.

Stevie nodded. "Hey."

Ana and Inez said quiet hellos.

"We've gotta blast," Morgan said, twisting her long, thick blonde hair into a messy bun on top of her head and fastening it with an elastic she pulled off her wrist. "Class starts in fifteen. You really should join us sometime."

"When they call it hot yoga, they aren't kidding," Monica added in a singsong voice filled with innuendo that made Stevie feel they were referencing some earlier conversation.

"Girl, I totally will," Farrah said.

Ana and Inez started to say goodbye, but Farrah stopped Inez, putting a hand of square-cut French-tipped nails on her forearm.

"Omigod, that coat is sooo cute on you."

It was a beautiful jacket. Stevie had actually noticed it earlier. A turquoise peacoat that was especially great with Inez's coloring. She knew Farrah's "cute" tricks, though, and waited for the insult the compliment would turn out to be.

"And I'm so, so glad it was you that got it. I mean, another academy connection. What a small world!"

Stevie froze.

"I just knew someone would be able to use it. I thought of bringing it to the Value Village downtown, but then I thought, just because we live in a ritzier area doesn't mean there aren't people in need right here. Am I right? So into New-To-You it went."

Inez's eyes snapped, but she didn't say anything. Ana looked as if she wanted to flee.

"I mean, the small bleach mark where I tried to remove nail polish is hardly noticeable. I mean, if it hadn't been my coat, even *I* wouldn't have noticed it."

Exactly as Farrah had no doubt planned, each of the four women's eyes followed her gaze. A pea-sized faded mark was suddenly super noticeable, although Stevie agreed with Farrah's initial observation: that if she hadn't pointed it out, no one would've noticed it.

Stevie had a whole rush of words she'd like to share, but she reined herself in, settling for, "Wow, Farrah . . . Just . . . *Wow*."

"What's that supposed to mean?" Farrah sounded wounded, as if Stevie was the one being rude.

"Take it however you want," Stevie said cheerily. She turned her back on Farrah and her cronies and spoke to Inez as if they were no longer there.

"That coat *is* amazing on you, and I'm glad you scored a deal. Only a complete idiot would pay the prices they ask for those jackets new."

"Thanks," Inez said dryly, "but I'm not so insecure that the opinions of the Farrahs of the world mean anything to me."

"Now I'm impressed," Stevie blurted, accidentally reverting to her say-whatever-she-thoughts self. "You are who I esteem to be! I hate it, but people like that always have the power to make me feel like crap."

"No," Inez said, the sharpness in her voice softening. "Only you have that power."

"Well—" Stevie broke off. "Actually, that's good food for thought. My mom Maddie would say similar."

Inez smiled. "I'm a nanny. Saying wise mother-like things is literally my job."

"I can tell you're worth every dime," Stevie said, not joking. "But speaking of which," she added as something that should've occurred to her much earlier struck her. "You're both nannies. Where are the kiddos? Surely, both sets of parents didn't take off non-instructional days from work."

Ana and Inez exchanged a look that only lasted a split second, but Stevie caught it.

"What?" she asked.

"They're at Carter de Vries' birthday party?" Ana said it as if it were a question.

Inez nodded.

Stevie wracked her brain, but she was so, so careful about making sure she kept up with papers and emails related to school or peer *anythings*.

"And what . . . all the kids in both classes were invited?"

Ana shifted from foot to foot. "Not all."

Clearly not, Stevie thought. "But most?" she said.

Ana nodded miserably.

"He's a brat. Be glad your Joey doesn't have to associate with him," Inez said.

That was all fine and good, Stevie thought. And on one hand, she wasn't worried. Joey had friends. He was well-liked —as he should be; he was beyond wonderful, funny, kind, thoughtful—but her heart hurt that he would be excluded when there was only one reason he would be. She didn't fit in with the Greenridge Young Learners Academy parents, so maybe they assumed her son didn't belong either.

It was still bothering her as she made her way through traffic toward Fox & Hound. Not that Joey hadn't been invited to the party. He'd be having a way better time with Jo and his cousins than he would've had at even the biggest blowout of a kids' party anyway. And not that she didn't fit in that well with the Academy parents. Despite her comment to Inez about other people having the power to make her feel bad, she'd also always recognized that as the bull—and trauma response—that it was. Stevie hadn't made it through everything she'd survived and gotten where she had by listening to the opinions of people who didn't care about her, even if it hurt sometimes.

No, what was bothering her was a thought that had leaped into her head from seemingly out of nowhere when she started the van. And now that her brain had articulated it so clearly, she could not deny the truth of it. I'm not happy with my life—but it's not my life that's the problem. It's me. Somewhere along the line, I've stopped being *me*. I'm compromising myself too much.

CHAPTER 4

Not even noon, but from the looks of the full parking lot, Fox & Hound was already hopping. Stevie had to circle the block twice to find a spot—and walking into the pub showed her initial read to be right on. Almost every table was full. That seemed the norm these days, though. From the time they opened for brunch at ten a.m. until they closed at midnight Sunday through Thursday and until two a.m. Friday and Saturday, they were slammed. They were so fortunate, but it was also . . . a lot.

She paused for a moment to take a deep breath and just enjoy the sights and sounds of one of her favorite places in the world. Her birth mom Marilyn always said walking into the Fox & Hound felt like stepping back in time, yet was somehow terrifically modern too, with its dark burnished plank floors, brick walls, brass accents, and heavy leather furniture. That it was like something out of a movie—and Stevie knew exactly what Marilyn meant. Even though she had the luxury of being in this wonderful place almost daily, it never failed to awe her. Especially at this time of year. With huge, *real* Christmas trees glowing in every corner and arrangements of greenery, ribbons, and glass balls sparkling on every heavy slab table . . . well, it was just . . . perfect. And it was hers and Jackson's—and Joey's, of course. It made Stevie want to pinch herself every single time she entered the building.

She mentally shook herself and shifted to work mode. The thought flitted into her head that she should change into cooking clothes, but it left just as quickly as it came. She'd be lucky if she even saw the kitchen today, let alone cooked anything. It was office work for her. Again, per usual.

She greeted the hostess, Melody, then held a finger to her lips and winked. Melody laughed her tinkling laugh, which was as light and pretty as her name—and a funny contrast with her gravelly low voice that always reminded Stevie of an aging rockstar.

"Your secret's safe with me, boss."

It was a super helpful agreement they'd arrived at some months ago. If the rest of the staff learned of Stevie's presence, she got called on to answer questions, help with this or that, and put out various fires—one time, a *literal* fire when some bacon fat flared up—that staff was fully capable of handling on their own. Needing uninterrupted time occasionally, Stevie arranged with Melody, who'd been with them since Day 1, to keep her arrival on the down low whenever she gave the signal. Then, once Stevie had the day's most urgent details handled, she always went out and chatted with each staff member and helped where needed.

Walking to the back, toward the office, a memory flared hot and beautiful as kasseri cheese flambeed in brandy: her and Jackson working hip-to-hip in the kitchen, little Joe safe in his play area, though really he was rarely in it, adopted as he was by every server and worker in the place. Those were the days, she thought. She was thrilled their business had taken off so well and surpassed all their early expectations. Of course, she was. But she hadn't known it would mean saying goodbye to what she'd loved most about their endeavor. Making delicious food that fostered connections between friends and family. Cooking. Creating. *Together*. Now it felt like she and Jackson were business owners, managers, not artists, not a couple joined by love and passion—

That was it. All the feelings and unease and unsureness that had been stewing within Stevie finally came together. She knew what she had to do.

Like a sign of affirmation, she saw a light glowing under the heavy oak office door and felt a dusting of happy anticipation, almost relief. Jackson was here. She could clear the air, and maybe they could steal five minutes to talk about their personal life. And then she heard him say something too low for her to hear—and an answering feminine laugh that she couldn't miss.

Her lightbulb moment dimmed, and she knocked—knocked on her own office door!—before entering.

"Come in."

Jackson looked confused when he saw it was her. "Why'd you knock?"

Why indeed?

She laughed without mirth. "I guess I kinda forgot where I was." She turned to the woman in her space, who was more of a fixture than a guest these days.

"Hey, Eloise. How goes the battle today?"

"Oh, so good, Stevie. So good! You'll be excited, but I'll skedaddle and let Jackson give you the updates."

Stevie sighed. It was impossible not to like Eloise. She used words like "skedaddle" in all seriousness and was genuinely as cheerful and enthusiastic as she seemed—excellent qualities in a restaurant manager. Two would be in excellent hands with her at the helm. Stevie just wished Eloise was as old and crotchety as some of her vocabulary instead of a strawberry blonde bombshell with a body like Jessica Rabbit and a brain that wouldn't be out of place in the reality TV show *Shark Tank*. She also wished it didn't make perfect sense that Eloise and Jackson spent as much time together as they did and then texted or phoned incessantly too. But as Stevie knew well, it was all part of getting a new place off the ground.

Eloise lifted her jam-packed messenger bag, holding it to her chest rather than slinging it over her shoulder. She lifted one hand off the bag briefly and waggled her fingers. "Okay, you two. Toodles!"

"Toodles!" Jackson called back, straight-faced, catching Stevie's eye. She had to bite her lip to keep from laughing.

When Eloise was gone, Stevie went over to where Jackson was sitting on one of the yoga balls they used as desk chairs and draped herself over his shoulders from behind.

"Oh, no—watch the hair," he said.

"Ha, ha, funny. But also, seriously, I'm really sorry about that."

"It's okay. I overreacted, and I'm sorry about *that*. Lately, I feel like—"

But whatever Jackson was going to say got cut off by his phone's insistent ring. He checked the display and winced. "Sorry, I need to take this."

Stevie sighed, removed her arms from his neck, and lightly kicked the other yoga ball over to the second desk. She tuned out Jackson's side of his phone conversation and was soon lost in the part of her job she still loved—menu planning. The festive vegetarian dishes she was considering made her stomach growl, and her favorite meal combo for this year consisted of all new-to-the-pub offerings—well, all new except for the garlicky Brussels. They served the same recipe with their steaks this time of year.

Starter: Whipped Brie with honey and sea salt and crusty bread
Main: Roasted Butternut Squash Risotto with fried sage
Garlicky Roasted Brussels Sprouts
Dessert: Pear and Almond Tart

Stevie had eaten each dish on its own, and each was drool-worthy, but she figured—just for research's sake, of course, she should have the whole meal one day this week to see how it all paired together.

"Damn!"

Jackson's volume and word choice yanked Stevie out of her imagined food reverie. His phone call had ended, and not well, apparently.

"What's up?" she asked.

"That was Bill. We can't get the flooring we want. And the kitchen supply guy was on site today. The stoves we need are backordered. They don't have an ETA."

Bill was the contractor in charge of their renovations. Stevie had wanted to keep and make do with the existing kitchen in the new location for the first year or two. Jackson, however, had thought it was better to bite the bullet and do all the necessary work at once so they didn't have to close for renovations in the near future and risk killing rising momentum for the new place. It had made sense, but now the kitchen was stripped.

"So, what does this all mean?"

"I need to go to Dawson."

"Now?" He'd only been back two nights after spending almost a week there, looking at paint, fabrics, windows, and the works.

"Yeah. If I go now, I'll still have a few hours before all the retailers close. It's possible some of the local furniture stores also have commercial lines. Not to mention the flooring. I need to put eyes on whatever alternatives we consider going with myself."

"You really can't just call around?"

Jackson looked pained, and Stevie knew why. They always got better service—and prices—face to face. It was too easy for an inexperienced salesperson to say, "No, sorry," to a cold call request—much more difficult when the customer was in earshot of their boss. And you really couldn't gauge the quality of materials from online photos.

Stevie lifted her face to Jackson. He gave her a dry peck, clearly already out the door in his mind.

"Drive safe," Stevie said. "And come back tonight?"

Jackson frowned like she'd asked something onerous. "I'll do my best."

He disappeared, leaving Stevie alone and disappointed. She'd wanted to run the Christmas specials past him too, but then she had an excellent idea. They'd be having a family night tomorrow, decorating the tree Jo and little Joe were hunting at this very moment. She'd choose a few of the most delicious items from their holiday menu and make them. Then she, Jackson, and Joey could feast while they decked the halls.

She returned to her task reinspired and ended up very pleased with the menu as a whole. Soon she had her grocery and liquor order placed too, and with Jackson taking care of further discussions with the contractor, she sent a first payment to Bill's company, then headed out of the office to see how the evening was shaping up in the pub.

No one had called in sick, the kitchen was at the top of their game foodwise, and everything was gleaming. Stevie always felt so proud of their team. They really were top-notch, to quote Eloise. She hung out for an hour, chatting with the servers, and then visited the kitchen staff and popped into the dish pit. Dinner service was just picking up when her phone rang. It was Jo.

"We have a huge favor to ask," she said after Stevie greeted her. In the background, Ollie and Grace chimed, "Pretty, pretty please," in unison. Stevie laughed, suspecting she knew what was coming.

"The crew wants to know if Joey can stay for dinner and sleep over. There's the Season of Giving meeting, as you know—you're coming, right?—but Luke says he's happy to watch them all."

"Oh, that would be perfect! Jackson had to run to Dawson to look at some stuff for the pub, and I don't know if he'll be back in time to watch Joey while I attend."

"It's settled then." Stevie could hear the smile in Jo's voice.

There was cheering in the background.

"You're sure it's really no trouble?"

"Definitely, no trouble. In fact, there might be mutiny if you said no at this point."

"And my tree isn't in your way?"

"Not at all. Luke was already planning to deliver it today or tomorrow, whichever worked easiest for you guys."

"You two are the best. Thank you," Stevie said, and then a little idea sprouted.

"Actually, what would you think if I skipped the meeting tonight? Would you mind terribly?"

"No, not at all, but why?"

"Inspiration just hit me. Jackson and I haven't had a night to ourselves in a very long time. Maybe I can call him and get him to hurry home."

Jo's rich laughter, one of Stevie's favorite sounds in the world, filled her ears. "Say no more. I mean it, really, please don't."

Stevie grinned into her phone but, as commanded, didn't say anything, and Jo continued, "But that's a fabulous idea. I'm glad this impromptu sleepover can aid and abet you."

A second of hesitation made Stevie pause before thanking Jo once more. She had promised Marilyn—

"And don't worry one bit about missing out on any information," Jo added. "As you know, I'm an excellent note-taker. I'll pass on every single thing you need to let Marilyn and Jamie know."

Stevie swallowed a lump that suddenly grew in her throat. "Thank you so much, Jo. I mean it. You always, always come through for me."

"Of course—just like you do for me, silly. It's what us soul sisters do."

"Yeah," Stevie agreed croakily.

This time, it was Jo who hesitated. Then she inquired, "Are you *sure* everything's all right? You're *really* okay?"

Like an idiot, Stevie nodded. She caught herself and forced words instead. "I'm fine. Honestly. Just tired, I think."

"Hm," Jo said, and Stevie could tell her sister was less than convinced.

They got off the phone, and Stevie crossed her fingers, then called Jackson. He sounded harried, and the background noise suggested he was in a busy store.

"Hey, baby," Stevie said in a corny, over-the-top, flirting voice. "Whatcha doing later?"

"What's up? What do you need?"

Stevie fought a feeling of hurt that seared through her.

"I'm . . . " She shook her head. "Sorry, I know you're trying to get a lot done before the shops close, but there's been a change of plans. Jo's keeping Joey for the night. I thought I'd blow off the fundraising meeting. If you hurry home, you and I could, I don't know . . ." Stevie had aimed to sound flirty again at the end there but didn't know if she pulled it off. Jackson was just so . . . awkwardly quiet. Why hadn't he interrupted her and said that was amazing and he'd be right home?

"Crap, I'm sorry. I've already booked a hotel room. I'm going to be a few hours yet, and I'm bushed. Besides, I need to be here again tomorrow. It doesn't make any sense for me to come back to Granite Ridge just to turn right back around."

Stevie shook her head and tried to keep her voice calm. "Why do you have to be there again tomorrow? You'll be back by the evening, right?"

"No, unfortunately, probably not. That's why I have to stay. A couple of nut jobs have organized a public meeting for citizens concerned about having a pub in their residential area. I want to go, make nice, and help them see the truth. Fox & Hound, a local pub with great food and family dining hours, will only enhance their neighborhood."

Stevie had only let Jackson carry on as long as he did because she was trying to get her temper under control, so she didn't scream—or burst into tears.

"But tomorrow is our family tree decorating day! Every year, it's the same day, Jackson. I've been talking about it for weeks. Joey picked out the trees today. I have the food planned—" Her voice caught.

Jackson's voice lowered. "Bad timing. I totally forgot." Stevie could practically hear what-to-do thoughts popping and sizzling in her husband's head. Finally, he sighed. "That's okay, we can do it the next day."

"No, Joey has school on Monday."

"So, we'll put the trees up on Sunday night and decorate them bit by bit through the week."

"That's not the same! That makes it feel like something we're fitting in."

"It *is* something we're fitting in."

"Jackson!"

"Okay, okay, we'll do it next weekend. Friday or Saturday. You pick. It'll be great."

"It's Season. Of. Giving. Next weekend," Stevie seethed. "And before you try to postpone again, then it's *Christmas*."

There was silence. Then Jackson spoke again, sounding frustrated. "I don't know what you want me to do."

I want you to come home to me, Stevie cried inside. *I want you to love me, to love Joey, to love us, more than that stupid effing second restaurant that I never wanted in the first place.*

She didn't say any of that, though, because she momentarily couldn't speak.

"Stevie?" Jackson finally said after the silence between them stretched.

"It's fine," she said dully. "We'll do it Sunday night. One late night won't kill him."

"That's my girl," Jackson said, and Stevie mimed vomiting even though she had no audience. When had he become *that* guy?

She said goodbye in as civil a tone as she could muster, but then, just before she hit End Call, she heard Eloise's voice in the background.

"What do you think of these?" Eloise chirped.

"Eloise is there? She went to Dawson with you?" Stevie said—or, more accurately, *shrieked*. Her heart hammered so hard in her chest that she thought for sure Jackson would hear it. It felt like she was bleeding. Why would he invite Eloise, not her, his wife and business partner? Or, at the very least, why hadn't he mentioned Eloise was accompanying him?

"Yeah, why?"

Stevie took a long, deep breath. It did nothing to calm her. "Unbelievable."

She hit End before he could make a lame excuse or act

like it was nothing and make her feel like she was crazy. Then she turned off her phone. She didn't want to hear him call and call and call or text and text and text.

And she definitely didn't want to hear dead silence from her phone if he *didn't* call or text.

CHAPTER 5

Even from the street, Granite Grinds, the coffeeshop that had graciously hosted the Season of Giving fundraising committee's meetings all year, was obviously packed. Its windows glowed cheery yellow in the dark night, and every time the green multipaned door opened, its string of bells tinkling, the rich scent of roasting beams wafted out along with a chorus of chatter and general merriment. It made Stevie feel lonely, the way she so often had as a kid, like no matter how hard she worked or how hard she tried, in some ways, she'd always be on the outside looking in.

How Stevie wished she could just turn tail and leave, but she didn't want to go home to her empty house. It had been depressing enough just going back to drop Syd off, feed him dinner, and change into clothes she was more comfortable in. And it would be sad enough sleeping in her bed alone. She'd almost crashed Jo's house to play with the kids but thought better of it. It was special for Joey, Grace, and Ollie to have pure cousin only time—and it wasn't fair to stick Jo with the task of reporting back to her if she didn't have a good reason.

She forced herself to cross the street and enter. Then she purchased a golden milk, hoping it would calm her and wanting to make sure she bought something because the coffee shop didn't charge the group for using the space.

One small mercy: she was a pinch late. Not so much that it would look bad, but enough that the event coordinator from Cedar Mountain Lodge had already started talking and was busy handing out instruction sheets for vendors, booth owners, and volunteers. Stevie collected one of each sheet passed her way, then took a seat near the edge of the group's circle, glad she wouldn't have to make small talk. She spotted Jo—who raised her eyebrows in silent question, no doubt wondering why she wasn't with Jackson as planned—and gave a little wave to her and to Gina, who was sitting beside her.

Stevie listened conscientiously to all the many, many bullet points and reminders, nodding in all the right places. The earliest anyone could set up was Friday. Check. Every booth needed to be removed—in full—by six p.m. on Sunday. She paid close attention to the locations for power on the provided map and mumbled "yes" along with everyone else at the stressed importance of adhering to the safety requirements for any extension cords and power strips. But all she wanted was for the meeting to be over. And it made her sad to be feeling so bah humbug about such a wonderful event.

After a few questions from the crowd that Stevie peevishly found irritating because they had been covered and covered to death, the coordinator handed out final copies of the program, where each cause's booth was highlighted, listing their website and ways people could donate to their cause even if they couldn't attend the event in person.

Despite her curmudgeonly mood, Stevie's spirit lifted.

The colorful brochure was beautiful—festive and fun and sure to pull Granite Ridgeans up the mountain to the lodge for the event.

Next, Stevie disciplined herself to listen as the coordinator yammered about their extensive social media and local advertising campaign in case she could pick up helpful tips for Fox & Hound.

No one clapped louder than Stevie when the ad the coordinator shared via the coffee shop's smart TV finished because, yes, it was fantastic, but also . . . the ad was the last point on the agenda. The meeting was over! Finally.

She gathered her papers, waved in Jo's direction, and practically sprinted out the door so no one could wrangle her into a conversation. She'd wait by Jo's SUV and see if she had time to visit. She was desperate to avoid small talk but equally desperately to *really* talk.

She walked until she found Jo's SUV, then took shelter in a covered entrance by a nearby closed-for-the-night clothing shop.

It was a good fifteen minutes before Jo's tall, shapely figure neared her vehicle, keys in hand. Stevie hadn't meant to sneak up on her, but Jo jumped like a boogie man was after her when Stevie appeared.

"Jo, it's okay! Sorry, it's just me."

Jo's hand flew to her heart. "You startled the pants off me! I thought you were long gone!"

Stevie couldn't help it. She laughed a little. "Nope, still here. I just didn't have it in me to socialize back there. Sorry. Any chance I can steal you for a few minutes to walk and talk?"

Jo didn't hesitate, and gratitude for her sister flooded through Stevie.

"Of course! Just let me shoot Luke a quick text and let him know I'll be a little late."

Jo typed rapidly, then grabbed a large scarf from the front seat of her SUV.

"Won't you get cold?" Jo asked, taking in Stevie's light-weight jacket and hoodie.

"No," she answered truthfully. "I'm too steamed to feel the temperature."

Jo laughed. "Steamed, not *pissed off*?"

"What can I say?" Stevie asked wryly. "Motherhood has irrevocably changed me—and cleaned up my potty mouth."

"Miracles do exist," Jo joked, but there was a softness in her tone, an awareness or something. Stevie could tell she didn't need to tell Jo something was wrong. Jo already knew. A warm blanket of reassurance wrapped around Stevie like a hug. It didn't matter how much of a fish out of water she felt sometimes; she was not alone—not anymore, never again. She had her sisters. She had family. She had—

Pain stopped that thought. It was always in the fore-ground of her mind to add Jackson to her list of people, but now...

They walked in silence for a block, Stevie assembling her thoughts and Jo letting her. Around them, the night was dark and cold, but the little storefronts surrounding Granite Grinds, though closed, were all decked out in Christmas lights. In any other circumstances, it would have felt merry and bright.

When Stevie finally spoke, it was like steam escaping from a pressure canner. Her words came out in a long, hot stream. She told Jo how tired she was lately and how little satisfaction and joy was taking in her work—how she missed just cooking. She explained her reservations about her and Jackson running two pubs in two different towns. A dash of lightness came back into her voice as she spoke about little Joe and how much she loved him and how amazing he was—but then the lightness was lost in the soup of her worries that she and Jackson wouldn't have enough time together with him. She shared how she didn't feel Joe's school was a good fit and how she didn't understand or agree with paying so much money for a kindergarten program.

Jo let Stevie vent without uttering a sound except for a gentle word of commiseration from time to time and occasional "Go on" noises.

And then Stevie got to the real crux of her heartache.

"I'm afraid I'm losing Jackson. Or that we're losing each other—" Saying the horrible words out loud scraped her throat. Made it ache.

Jo, usually the embodiment of calm, let out a sharp, surprised gasp.

Stevie stopped walking abruptly, bit her lip, and shot Jo a look. "I know. It's bad, right? I can't even pinpoint exactly what it is or when it started going bad. Maybe unhappiness just sneaks up? I just feel like whatever I do, it's not enough. It's like he doesn't see me anymore."

A memory of the don't-mess-my-hair moment flared in her mind for a second. "Or maybe that's not fair. It's like . . . I don't know. We keep missing each other. He'll try to connect; I'll blow it. I keep trying to send him signals. He'll miss every single one, almost like intentionally, it seems."

"I feel like a terrible sister. I had no idea things weren't still good between you guys."

Stevie shook her head. "You are the exact opposite of that."

"Still . . . just lately, I picked up there was something going on with you, but I would never have guessed this. How long has it been? Please tell me not since the beginning?"

"No, no, not even close. That's what makes it so difficult. I can't deny something's wrong because I know what we're like when we're right. But I don't know . . . it's like the first five years or so were all happy hormones, new baby bliss, and new business buzz, and somehow . . . maybe the rush of hormonal joy slowed, and busyness pushed the bliss for him aside." She paused, and Jo nodded, looking contemplative in the soft glow of Christmas lights that shone around them.

"Anyway." Stevie gave a big exhale. "The bigger thing with us is that if you don't work on yourself, face your past, heal your traumas, you'll unconsciously relive them in your other relationships. You won't even know you're doing it."

Jo looked a little surprised or something, and Stevie let out a wry laugh. "I know, I know. Who am I, right? It's Marilyn's influence. She gave me a bunch of books that she found helpful, thinking I might too."

And the books *had* been super helpful. What Stevie didn't tell Jo but might one day, if it came up, was how Marilyn had talked about attachment wounds, what they looked like, and how she was so sorry because she felt she'd probably hurt Stevie in a lot of the ways some of the books discussed. It had been incredibly painful but so, so healing and helpful. Both Marilyn's candidness and the literature.

Jo's breath made white puffs in the rapidly cooling air. "So, you think in the beginning, the exciting rush of new love was enough to compensate, but now maybe unresolved stuff from Jackson's past is coming up?"

"I don't know, but I think, maybe, yeah. It's like he's dead set on becoming his dad or some version of "success," at least, that his dad would recognize." Stevie gave a sad shrug. "And I'm consciously trying to make sure I don't make the same mistakes as Marilyn did or I did as a kid. I used to be so desperate for love, so desperate to feel any sense of safety, that I'd accept any scraps, beg for them, in fact."

"And now?" Jo's voice was soft as brushed velvet.

Stevie laughed a tad bitterly. "Well, little Stevie's a grown woman now—and you've seen me eat. I want a full meal with appetizers, desserts, and drinks. No scraps. That's what I tell my inner child. No more scraps, punk kid. You're better than that."

"Yes, you are—and I'm so proud of you. You were awesome as a 'punk kid' too, though. Remember, I knew you then as well."

Stevie smiled at that. "Thanks, sis. You're being too kind as usual." Then she winced. "There's something else, Jo."

Jo waited patiently as Stevie took a deep breath, and then shared her concerns about Eloise. "And I don't know. I really don't think they're having an affair, but my gut keeps saying *yet*. They're not having one *yet*. I don't want to be that woman. Insecure, laying down the law about not having female friends, etc.—but I don't like it. It doesn't feel safe."

Jo's beautiful, kind face furrowed in sadness. "Aw, Stevie. That absolutely . . . I don't know. For once, words fail me."

Stevie's sinuses prickled, and her eyes burned. "I know. Like I said earlier, it's bad, right?"

"Do you know what you're going to do?"

They'd reached the end of the shopping district now, and without discussing it, they turned back the way they'd come. After a few steps, Stevie laughed sadly and answered Jo's question. "There's really only one thing I can do, right?"

Jo waited.

"I have to work harder. Do more. Try to fit in better. Mold myself to be the perfect upscale wife. A wife befitting Jackson Elmsworth Bassett." Stevie said the last bit with a snooty, highbrow accent.

It was Jo's turn to stop walking abruptly. She stared at Stevie in disbelief.

"Ha! Don't worry. That was a joke." All traces of humor deserted Stevie, and she became grim again. "I have to talk to him—tell him all this, don't I?"

Jo nodded.

"I'm just scared, Jo. I love him so much, and I'm afraid . . ." Stevie's voice trailed off.

"Afraid of?" Jo prodded gently after a few beats had passed.

"That if I tell him how I really feel, that if I explain how unseen and unheard I feel, how I feel I'm living a life that doesn't work for me . . . he'll say he doesn't love me, he'll leave me."

Jo's face scrunched with empathy, and guilt seeped through Stevie. She hated that she was making Jo feel bad at Christmas. *No*, she said sternly in her head. *Jo loves you. She'd want you to bring this to her. Just like you would if your roles were reversed.* She nodded to herself, knowing her inner voice was true and feeling her nervous system calm down again.

"I'm sorry that you're going through all this—especially at Christmas," Jo said, and Stevie smiled despite herself. Another thing she and her older soul sister shared. A huge love of Christmas—for all the usual reasons, she supposed, but also knowing for them it went deeper than the presents, food, and fun the season represented. Christmas was also the precious anniversary of them becoming a family. And it was Stevie's wedding anniversary week too. She was punched back to sadness again.

"I feel like I'm on this constant see-saw, so grateful and happy for so many things in my life, but so frustrated and sad and scared at the same."

"That's super hard," Jo agreed. "When are you going to talk to him?"

Stevie let out a loud, frustrated sigh. "That's the tricky part. It's Christmas. We're slammed at Fox & Hound, which is awesome but also means we're stretched thin. Things are coming to a boil with Two, and there always seems to be some detail or other that needs to be attended to. There's the Season of Giving—" She broke off and sighed again, less explosively this time, more contemplatively. "And all this explains exactly why Jackson and I are in the stew we're in, doesn't it?"

Jo tilted her head questioningly.

"If there's no time—or willingness—to address the problems now, it shows we didn't have time, or were no longer making time, to do the things that kept building us and maintaining us and growing us *together*."

"That's a danger zone for all of us, isn't it?" Jo said, her voice thoughtful and sympathetic. "Life is really busy. But Jackson loves you, Stevie. I know he does. I think you guys can find your way back to each other."

Stevie's stomach felt like dough that had been over-kneaded. "I really hope so," she said. "But also, you and I both know that sometimes love isn't enough."

Jo took Stevie's hand, gripping it hard, and Stevie knew she understood all too well. After all, life had shown them both, in very hard ways, that sometimes love did die. Sometimes it did fail. Platitudes and wishful thinking didn't change this hard truth.

"And yet, there's always other love to count on and rely on," Jo said softly. She was still holding Stevie's hand, and Stevie squeezed it back.

"Absolutely." Stevie's heart panged, though. She was blessed to have the steady love of her sisters, moms, little Joe, etc. But she wanted Jackson, her husband, to love her and care for her and be invested in her, in *them*, the way he'd vowed to. And she hadn't been lying to Jo. She was afraid. Afraid he'd decided she wasn't enough for him, that he wanted someone fancier, with a similar background and goals, etc. She couldn't bear to lose him—but she might have to. It would be worse to only keep him if doing so meant she had to completely abandon herself. If he only stayed with her because it was easier for him, not because he truly loved her . . .

They were almost back at their vehicles, and Stevie shivered, suddenly feeling the cold.

"Will you be okay tonight?" Jo asked.

"Yep," Stevie said. "I'm a survivor."

"Always," Jo agreed. She seemed about to say something else but then shook her head and hugged Stevie instead. "I love you, little sister."

"I love you too. And thanks so much for listening to me bellyache."

"Not bellyaching—and anytime. I mean it."

Stevie knew she did and felt her stupid eyes mist up yet again.

While she always missed Hailey, who lived in Florida and was busy with her own family, and Alissa, who was away again this year for the holidays and traveled more and more with Jed for his business ventures, Jo was an ever-steady rock and source of friendship and support. Stevie was so, so grateful for her.

"I hope you know I'd do anything for you, Jo," she said seriously.

Jo laughed, but her voice was serious too. "I do know that. Thank you."

They firmed up a time for little Joe and the trees to be dropped off the next day, and Stevie asked Jo if the Wednesday after the Season of Giving, so just before Christmas weekend, worked for their annual family Christmas-goodies-baking day."

"Are you sure in light of everything—"

"I'm absolutely sure," Stevie interrupted. "It's our tradition, and it's important. I'm sorry I left planning it so late this year."

"Okay," Jo said, sounding unsure. "But let me host it at my

house—and promise me that if it's too much or if after talking to Jackson it doesn't work for some reason, you'll cancel or postpone even if it's last minute."

"Deal."

After saying their goodbyes, Stevie sat in her van without driving long after its engine was warm and Jo had rumbled off in her SUV. Even with Syd waiting for her, the prospect of returning to an empty house made her feel empty too.

CHAPTER 6

Saturday morning, Joey bounded into the house, Ollie and Grace on his heels. Syd skipped around in circles of delight at seeing his boy again. Stevie knew exactly how her little dog felt, and she picked Joey up and squeezed him tight when she said hello. She didn't need to ask if he'd had a good time. He was chatting a mile a minute, sharing every detail of his Christmas tree hunt—a sleigh ride with real horses being the highlight, apparently—and pizza night.

Stevie hugged her niece and nephew hello too. Jo and Luke trailed in after the kids, Stevie holding the door open for them and the trees they bore: a small one by Jo and a seven-foot Noble Fir by Luke.

"What's this?" Stevie asked, motioning at the mini tree.

"It's one for me!" Joey chortled. "For my room, just like Ollie and Gracie!"

"Wow! You're so lucky!" Stevie said.

"Yeah!" Joey high-fived his mom.

"I hope it's all right?" Jo said.

"It's awesome," Stevie assured her.

Jackson? Jo mouthed silently over the kids' heads.

"Not a word yet," Stevie whispered barely above breath to avoid being heard by the kids. Jo winced, and her eyes carried questions Stevie felt sure were mirrored in her own.

"Mommy, Mommy! Can we decorate the trees now, and can Ollie and Gracie stay to help, and can we have snacks and—"

"Whoa, tiger," Stevie said, laughing and appreciating the respite from her thoughts. "I think Auntie Jo and Uncle Luke have plans today, but you and I can do some fun Christmassy stuff until Daddy gets home tomorrow. We'll decorate the trees then."

"Can we please play here for just a little while?" Grace begged as if it had been years since she'd gotten to visit her younger cousin instead of the tail end of a 24-hour visit.

"Maybe just half an hour. I know you guys are play-time deprived," Luke said, winking, then adding to Stevie and Jo, "I thought we could help get the trees set up at least, so it's one less thing you need to do before decorating."

"Great idea," Jo agreed.

Stevie had to smile. "You guys are too much, but don't get me wrong! I accept all free labor so long as I can send you home with a couple of frozen meals."

"It's the only reason we offered to help—the hope for one of your lasagnas," Luke joked.

"I knew it!"

Jo shook her head at both of them.

A little while later, Stevie and Joey were waving enthusiastic goodbyes out the front window and pulling funny faces, making their departing cousins giggle as they waved back, walking backward toward their SUV. The house was filled with the crisp, outdoorsy scent of fresh pine and sweet chocolate because Stevie had agreed with Joey that they needed hot cocoa. They spent a quiet day playing and watching Christmas movies.

Sunday, Stevie went into the pub to help with brunch, which was always a busy time for them. Then, happy when all the afternoon shift had shown up, she headed home again with Joey.

By five, a soft snow had started to fall, much to Joey's glee, several stories had been read, and Stevie had caved and put strings of white lights on both the tree in the living room and the little one in Joey's bedroom. Jackson was still nowhere to be seen and hadn't replied to any of Stevie's calls or texts. She wanted to stay present with Joey, to enjoy every little moment with him until Christmas decorating, yet her attention wandered more and more.

"Can I hang things on my tree now? Pretty, pretty, please?"

Stevie suspected that since "pretty, pretty, please" was Grace's new phrase, she'd be hearing it a lot out of Joey's mouth. It made her smile. She, Jo, Alissa, and Hailey had often emulated each other's ways of talking, and if someone came home from school with a new catchphrase, they all seemed to adopt it.

Joey tugged her arm. "Please? I want the dinosaur ones!"

The *dinosaur ones*. Last year, Stevie, Jackson, and Joey had stumbled upon a set of what looked like old 50s-style foil ornaments but were all different types of dinosaurs in Santa hats and roller skates. They'd all been completely smitten, and though their price tag was a bit shocking, Stevie, with her love of eclectic Christmas ornaments and her own impressive personal collection going back to childhood, was adamant they were a need, not a want, which had made Jackson laugh hard. The memory made her check her phone again, even though she knew full well no call or text from Jackson had slipped by unnoticed.

"The dinosaur ones it is, little man. And some candy canes?"

"Yes!"

Stevie wasn't worried that Joey would sneak them behind her back and eat too much sugar. He had her tastebuds, not Marilyn's.

She lost herself in the happy world of tree decorating with her boy and made them tomato soup and grilled cheese sandwiches for dinner. And not fancy grilled cheese with Gruyere or Muenster, either. Classic old American cheddar. The only way to do it.

"Yum!" Joey exclaimed happily. "Just like Gramma's."

"Exactly!" Stevie pressed a kiss to the top of her son's head as she returned to the table after grabbing the ketchup. Marilyn's grilled cheese and tomato soup meals were one of a handful of truly happy memories from Stevie's youngest days, a simple but perfect combo that always felt like the best part of home. Whatever else might be going on in your life, when you're eating grilled cheese and soup, you're cozy and safe.

She let Joey have an extra-long bubble bath before bed.

He'd been asleep for almost two hours when she heard the purr of Jackson's Audi A5 in the driveway, then the click of the deadbolt turning as he entered the unlock code. Her husband was home.

Stevie rose from the living room couch, where she'd been half drowsing, half perusing a food magazine, and padded to the entranceway to greet him, bringing the blanket she was wrapped in with her.

Jackson's back was toward her, and he was placing his coat in the closet. As he turned around, Stevie bit back the sharp words she wanted to greet him with. Dark shadows smudged his eyes, and he hadn't shaved. His shirt was rumpled, and if she could be trusted to notice a detail like this, she was pretty sure it was the same one he'd been wearing when he left for Dawson two days ago. And his hair looked almost greasy. For someone as meticulous about his appearance as Jackson was, this was akin to . . . Oh, heck, Stevie didn't know. Something bad, anyway. He looked terrible.

"Hey," she said softly. "You okay?"

He startled like she was a ghost or something and shook his head, then nodded, scrubbing at his stubbled jaw. "No, yeah. I'm fine. It's just been a really long day."

"Can we talk?"

The question was like grease on a fire, and Jackson's whole countenance changed. He erupted. "Can't you ever give it a rest? I just said I'm exhausted!"

Stevie took a step back, and Jackson looked chagrined. As abruptly as his anger sparked, it died out. "I'm sorry."

"We say that too much these days. It's basically meaningless."

They glared at each other, and Stevie swallowed against the hard lump in her throat.

Jackson muttered an expletive under his breath. "Can it at least wait until tomorrow?"

"Fine." But it wasn't fine. It was definitely—everything was definitely—the opposite of *fine.*

Jackson strode away from her, then stopped and stood stock-still, staring with horror into the living room.

"Christmas tree decorating. I totally, totally forgot."

"Apparently."

Stevie pushed past him, head down, not wanting him to see her tears.

Maybe he did see them, though, because he called after her, his voice resentful, like asking to chat was asking for the moon. "I said tomorrow, not next year! Surely, it's not too much to ask that you wait one bloody day to get everything sorted."

CHAPTER 7

B ut tomorrow came, and they did not "get everything
sorted." It was a Monday from H. E. double hockey
sticks. Joey woke up with a fever and scratchy
throat. The chef and sous chef both called in sick, and they
had two Christmas parties booked. In addition to the regular
merry mayhem this time of year, Stevie figured that would
make for a full house from 11:00 a.m. till close. The cute
carrot-shaped bags Stevie had purchased to hold the pre-
mixed dry soup bases they'd be selling for Season of Giving
hadn't arrived, so she'd need to source a different container
locally.

She and Jackson exchanged perfunctory good mornings
and, out of necessity, swung into business team mode. Stevie
called Joey's school and said they'd be keeping him home for
the day, and since there were only two more days before the
Christmas break, she said he'd be absent for those days as
well. Then she called Maddie.

"Hey, sweetie! What's cooking?" Maddie's melodious
voice—and the inside joke, since Stevie had been cooking

ever since Maddie showed her how, immediately soothed Stevie. Her beloved foster mom had never seen a challenge she couldn't handle with grace and strength. From losing her husband and daughter in a horrible accident, to taking on not one but four girls who needed homes and forging a new family, to bravely opening up to love again once she was an empty nester—and then facing the surprise that she'd had a biological half-sister who'd been a secret all of her life— Maddie seemed to use every hardship to learn, grow, and show love. And she wasn't just Stevie's hero and ultimate role model. Each of Maddie's daughters of her heart, as Maddie herself referred to them, felt the same way.

Apparently, Stevie paused too long because Maddie spoke again, "Stevie, are you there?"

"Sorry, yeah. I was just thinking how much I love you."

"Aw, lovely girl. I love you too. Is everything okay?"

The fact that everyone in her life who cared about her kept asking her that—except her husband, the one person who she wished would—wasn't lost on Stevie.

She shook her head but said, "Yeah, yeah, just a bit chaotic." She wasn't lying to Maddie. She just didn't have time to discuss her marriage right now, and honestly, she needed to know exactly what was up before she worried her.

"I was wondering if you could perhaps watch Joey today and tonight. Maybe have him for a sleepover?" Stevie briefly explained the day's events.

"Oh, shoot! I'd love nothing more than a day with Joey, but I'm actually away in Boise. I came up here for the weekend to help Lindsey get some things packed for the condo and to help her with holiday gifts for her clinic staff. In fact, she's at the clinic now, and I'm at her house on craft duty making holiday gifts."

Stevie loved her no-longer-a-secret aunt—and loved that

Maddie had her own soul sister now even more—so she was being completely genuine when she said, "That's great! Have fun."

"Will you be able to figure something out?"

"Absolutely."

"Okay . . . well, if you don't, call me back, and I'll just tell Lindsey I have to head home. I could always just drive back up here tomorrow to help her."

"No. It's fine."

"All right. But you call me if you need me to come, okay? If I don't hear from you, I'll see you at Cedar Mountain Lodge for the Season of Giving, if not before."

"You bet."

Stevie got off the phone and moved on to Plan B, still feeling awed that not only was this next call possible, but she had absolutely no qualms about it.

Marilyn answered on the first ring. "Stevie! Hello, good morning! What a treat to hear from you!"

"Hey, Mom. Good morning to you too." Stevie laughed self-consciously, feeling honored and, as ever, a bit overcome by how happy Marilyn always was to hear from her, like she couldn't quite believe her luck.

"What's up?"

Stevie recited the same tale of morning adventure woes she'd shared with Maddie and then repeated her need for a babysitter.

"Are you kidding? I'd love to! My place or yours? Which is easier for you?"

Marilyn acted like Joey's virus and an emergency call to see if she could babysit was a divine gift. Stevie grinned despite the knot of nerves tying and untying in her stomach, and her heart ached a little. Marilyn really was awesome. She was so grateful to have her back in her life, to really *have* her.

And now, with six years of sobriety under Marilyn's belt, Stevie often felt like it could even last.

"Are you sure you're not just being overly accommodating? I know you, Jamie, and John have a lot to get done before you head up to Cedar Mountain Lodge this weekend, and speaking of which, that reminds me—" Stevie explained the soup mix bag dilemma.

"First things first, I'm thrilled to have a full day with Joey and Syd—and Mille will be over the moon too—well, not that she can jump very high these days, but she wishes."

Stevie laughed out loud at the reference to her petite mother's ginormous, aged Newfoundlander dog, whose heart was as big as her body.

"And secondly, that's great news about the bags!"

"Uh huh," Stevie said drily. She'd become used to the often-over-the-top positivity that people in recovery sometimes seemed to possess. The most mind-blowing part of it was that usually, the more you got to know the chipper person, the more you realized their joy and positivity were genuine. A beautiful side benefit of doing all the work on themselves that helped them stay sober, Stevie figured.

"I'm serious."

"I know you are—but why?"

"Nell and I were helping a regular clean out his apartment that had gotten too full for him to manage."

Stevie was one hundred percent sure this gentle description meant the man in question was a hoarder and that "by too full to manage," Marilyn meant the guy had the place crammed to the rafters and the door barely opened.

"Yes, it was very full," Marilyn added in that uncanny way she had of seeming to read what you were thinking, though you hadn't said a word. "Anyway, the primary thing he has a penchant for is glass jars with lids. We took out hundreds of them, literally—all meticulously clean and boxed up. I'll run them through the commercial dishwasher in the kitchen, and then we can fill them there as planned—just with different containers. It's a win-win."

Stevie shook her head, smiling yet again. "Everything's a win-win with you."

"Right? I'm so fortunate."

They agreed that Marilyn would camp out at Stevie and Jackson's. That way, there was no pressure for specific pick-up or drop-off times. Relief trickled through Stevie as she got off the phone.

She went to check on Joey, who had fallen back into a sweaty sleep, his dark curls plastered to his little flushed head. She kissed his precious forehead and clicked off the TV. Then she rethought it and clicked it back on, lowering the volume. She'd always found the noise of the television soothing as a kid.

She glanced into the bedroom and their home office on her way to the kitchen but saw no sign of Jackson. Cocking her head to listen, no shower noise came from the master bath or the main washroom. A note on the butcher block cutting board on their island explained why.

Saw J was sleeping again and heard you on the phone handling things. I've gone into F&H to start getting the day sorted prep-wise. See you there.

No greeting. No word of affection. No acknowledgment of all the things piled up between them right now.

Was this how relationships died? Not in loud, noisy fights, but in cold, ever-deepening silences?

Stevie felt like her heart was literally bleeding, but that didn't soften the steel rod of certainty that suddenly ran up her spine.

I don't want to lose him. I don't want to lose him. I love him, one part of her cried.

You can love someone and *let them go if you have to*, another part of her replied firmly. *What you can't do is live in a one-sided relationship, gaslighting yourself. Whatever happens, you will be okay.*

Stevie knew it was true, but it wasn't comforting at all.

CHAPTER 8

The rest of the week sped past in a blur of covering shifts as the chef and sous chef's flu or whatever it was persisted. Inez's sister Callie proved worth her weight in gold, and Stevie scolded her lightly for applying for the dishwasher position or even considering prep cook work, promoting her officially to sous chef after just a couple shifts of working with her. Slow hours between lunch and dinner coverage were filled with compiling soup materials and filling jars for the Season of Giving. Thankfully, Joey was only sick one day and was happy to keep Stevie and Jackson company at the Fox & Hound. He still had his own little play area, complete with a TV, from his years before kindergarten, but now, as he had then, he preferred to be showing off for the staff and "helping."

And even more thankfully, Thursday night, when Stevie checked in with her sick staff members, both the chef and other sous chef said they were up to snuff. Fingers crossed, the rest of the staff stayed well until the weekend was over!

Jo checked in mid-week to see how Stevie and Jackson's

talk had gone, and Stevie was ashamed of her gutlessness but fessed up.

"I will talk to him. I'm not putting everything off indefinitely. I promise. I just need to wait until the Season of Giving is over. If I wreck Christmas, fine. Well—I'll be careful not to wreck it for Joey. But I have too many people counting on me for the fundraiser. I can deal with whatever comes if it's just my own holiday happiness I jeopardize, not other people's."

"Who is this cool-headed, practical-to-a-fault person, and what did she do with my fiery, passionate sister?"

Stevie laughed wryly. "Oh, don't worry. She's burning on the inside. This is just a temporary respite."

"Good," said Jo vehemently. "She is—you are—awesome. And it's making me angry that Jackson seems to have forgotten that. Any more news on the whole Eloise angle?"

The rock that was Stevie's stomach these days thudded painfully. "Nothing I can really point to one way or the other. And everything keeps going south with Two. It actually makes sense for him and her to be joined at the hip right now."

Jo made an irritated sound that Stevie's heart echoed.

"Okay, well, promise me you really will talk to him before Christmas and that if you need anything in the meantime, any hour, you call me."

Stevie promised.

Saturday morning, early, Stevie loaded the van with the tools she'd need for big batch soup building, including four 6-gallon pots that belonged to Pioneer soup kitchen, which John had dropped off the night before. Fox & Hound had similar pots, of course, but this time of year, they couldn't be spared. She was just packing the last of the coolers of pre-chopped ingredients when Jackson came outside and stood by the van door.

"Why do you have to bring all this up? I thought John had a van for the soup kitchen now?"

"He does, but it's filled to bursting with all the jars of pre-mixed soups we're going to sell. Wait till you see them! They turned out so cute! Nell trimmed them each with Christmas ribbon too."

Jackson shifted uneasily, and Stevie suddenly noticed he was wearing suit shoes, dress slacks, and a crisp suit shirt under his winter coat. Not exactly lodge attire.

She waited.

He cleared his throat. "I know I said I'd be able to help out this weekend, but I don't think it's going to work." He launched into a lengthy description of some new hiccup in the new location's plan. Apparently, what had made him so late the previous week was that the community meeting opposing a pub in the neighborhood had also revealed there was an old oil tank beneath the existing structure. They weren't disturbing the ground, so Stevie didn't see how it was that big a deal or how it could be an environmental hazard, but she wasn't one of the powers that be.

Stevie felt sympathy for him as Jackson doused her with the latest stressful details. Getting Two up and running and starting a successful "chain" meant a lot to him, and it was going badly.

She held up a hand to stave off any further explanations or excuses, however. "It's okay," she said softly. "Between me, Marilyn, Jamie, John, Nell, and Owen, we'll have it covered."

"What about Joey?"

"He's in his seat already. Syd too." Stevie motioned to the van's interior. "They're watching Paw Patrol. You can pop your head in and give him a kiss."

Jackson shook his head. "No, I mean, who will watch him?"

The question confused her. Who always watched Joey and organized everything for him?

She felt deeply sad. "His whole village will be up there, except you," she said softly. "He'll have a blast. Don't worry."

"Oh yeah, that makes sense. Okay then." Jackson gave a seemingly satisfied nod.

Stevie tried to smile but suddenly felt overwhelmingly tired on top of sad. "Okay, well . . . I should get going. The soups need a good four hours to simmer, and I've got a lot to do before people start arriving."

"Right, right."

"Kiss?" she asked, trying and failing not to feel pathetic for having to ask.

Jackson leaned in, but as ever these days, Stevie could tell he was already far away, putting out distant fires, barely aware of her as she grazed his mouth with hers. Could a person literally feel when their heart broke? She thought maybe, yes.

CHAPTER 9

In the eight years that Stevie had lived in her vintage RV, traveling and cooking her way across the country and extensive parts of Canada before marrying Jackson, she had seen more than her share of breathtaking views and mind-blowing scenery.

Without exaggeration, however, the trip up to Cedar Mountain Lodge was one of the most gorgeous drives Stevie had ever experienced—especially in winter. And this year was no exception. Every tree was draped in crystal-studded robes, and the sun, just starting its ascent, was turning the sky bright mauve behind the distant mountain ranges. And when she pulled into the lodge's big parking area, Joey was as delighted as she was. He let out a wonder-filled gasp, taking in the towering snow-draped cedars and massive mountains that flanked the magnificent lodge and surrounding ski village. It was as if it was his first visit to the lodge, not a place he'd come to multiple times a year his whole young life. Stevie knew how her son felt, though. This place always felt like magic to her too, no matter how often she visited.

She half turned in her seat to smile at her little boy,

marveling at how his beautiful brown eyes—Jackson's eyes—shone just as brightly as the dazzling array of Christmas lights strung everywhere around them.

"We're here! Are you excited?"

"Yes!" he cheered. "But remember, I get to make the soup. I will put in the ingredients. You can tell me how."

She grinned, her heart both full and heavy at the same time. As she observed so often, he was so her and Jackson's child in every way. What other five-year-old, when faced with the delights of a Winter Festival, was most excited about the chance to stir soup?

"Sounds like a plan. But first, we have to take Syd to doggy daycare."

As they walked toward the glowing lodge, little Joe's mittened hand in hers, Syd prancing along deer-like beside them, a passing van slowed. A window rolled down.

"Hey, don't I know you from somewhere?" called a cheery voice.

"Gramps!" Joey yelled enthusiastically, and once more, Stevie's heart filled. She and Marilyn had lived such a solitary existence, but her son really did have, like she'd said to Jackson, a village.

Maddie, aka Nana. Robert, aka Pops.

Marilyn, his Gramma. Her husband, the gentle giant Jamie, who was Gramps.

Three aunts, plus assorted aunts by affection.

Three uncles.

A plethora of cousins.

And the wealth wasn't just her son's.

How on earth had Stevie gone from a family, such as it was, of two to this utter wealth of loved ones? It was humbling and more than a little mind-blowing. She, who'd never had a dad, now had not one but two stepdads, both wonderful. She also had a dad-in-law, but as far as he'd come,

Mr. Bassett was still . . . Mr. Bassett. Stevie just avoided calling him anything personal most of the time to sidestep the awkward fact that he was not . . . Dad. Usually, she and Jackson arranged some sort of Christmas get-together with him. This year, however, back in early November, when Jackson tried to pre-book plans, Mr. Bassett had looked blank, then surprised.

"Oh," he said. "I thought I told you. I'm going to Belize for three months. I won't be here."

The hurt that flashed across Jackson's face before he managed to conceal it had made him look like little Joe to Stevie. She often thought that the lack of healing between Jackson and his dad, regardless of some of the progress that had legitimately been made, explained a lot about her husband, especially surrounding his desire to create an empire to prove something to his father, rather than just be content with a pub that was doing marvelously and provided for all their needs.

In another minute, Jamie had parked, and his brother John had pulled in behind him, along with their father, Owen, and his wife, Marilyn's surrogate mother, Nell. Soon, they were a loud, chatting crowd on their way to drop off the dogs—three between the families: Syd, Millie, and the chihuahua Pip. Next, they collected the tons of soup-related stuff and made their way toward the spot on the map that showed their space.

Jamie, John, and Owen had been up to the lodge the night before during the allotted times and had set up the booth and rigged the electrical cords Stevie needed for the portable induction cooktops. All they had to do today was get the food on, the dry soups displayed, and the booth decorated. *All.* The thought made Stevie laugh. It was actually a lot, but it was totally doable and felt very festive. Plus, she was in her element, cooking huge vats of homey, happy food for a crowd.

The lodge had supplied tables for each booth, but that was it. Stevie quickly threw green checked tablecloths over them and got busy plugging in the stove elements they'd brought. Marilyn and Nell started making a display for the dry soups. The menfolk busied themselves stringing lights and hanging the beautiful folk art sign Marilyn had created. And all the while, Joey flitted back and forth like a manic Christmas fairy, helping here, questioning there, and making them all laugh frequently.

All the soup prep went smoothly. Soon, tomatoey, garlicky, oniony goodness filled the air. More than one vendor hurried over to get a bowl before the event started. Time passed in a wink, but just before the Season of Giving opened to the public, Stevie took Joey on a tour of the booths —all so merry and fun, all for such good causes.

They made wreaths at Jo's booth and added them to the decoration of their own stall, already excited about how they'd look back at home.

Joey got his face painted like a Christmas cat—just a normal cat, but with a plush red Santa hat that they also provided—at a booth raising funds for one of the pre-schools in town.

They booked a time to return later with Syd to get Christmas pictures taken with him and Santa at Jo's sister-in-law Gina's stall.

There were various booths inside the lodge too, one of which was Sunset Paws Pet Hospice. They got hugs from Maddie and Lindsey, petted the elderly cats and dogs looking for homes, and made a donation.

Back outside, they did about a hundred other things too, including mingling with Winterfest's famous elves, who seemed to be everywhere, delivering coffee, cocoa, and cookies—all of which smelled delicious in the frosty air—to the guests and vendors. Joey was wide-eyed and almost speechless with wonder at it all.

The day, long before over and before even one donation had been counted, was already a roaring success, except for one missing element: Jackson. How could he not see that he was missing the best things in life?

Sunday passed even more quickly than Saturday, and they actually ran out of soup an hour or two before the event closed for the day. That was okay, though. It was way better than having gallon upon gallon of leftovers. They'd almost sold out of the dried soups too. Only ten jars of what Stevie fondly called Lovely Lentil remained. And just as quickly as the day passed, the whole busy, festive tent town that made up the Season of Giving was just . . . gone. Stevie was always surprised by how quickly tear down for events like this went, and she never quite understood why, but it always made her feel a little blue. It had been fantastic, though, with every vendor expressing grateful awe at how generous the attendees had been. Talk was already in the air about doing a Season of Giving event next year.

With all the vans loaded and ready for the return to Granite Ridge, the Pioneer Street Soup Kitchen crew decided to have dinner in the lodge before collecting their dogs from the doggie daycare and heading back down the mountain.

"I feel like my legs are going to fall off," Joey exclaimed as he settled into one of the deep leather chairs in the lodge's main restaurant. The whole group laughed, and Jamie and Owen let out grunts.

"You said it, boyo. Mine too," Owen agreed, his bright blue eyes twinkling.

"Lightweights," Stevie teased, and Marilyn and John grinned.

"What she said," John added. "Some of you have never spent twelve hours a day on your feet in a kitchen, and it shows."

They ordered, and the group fell into a happy, casual conversation about the build-up to Christmas and what the upcoming week held for each of them. Stevie sipped a hot mulled cider, listened to the chatter, and quietly soaked in the atmosphere. Mostly, though, she tried to breathe. Now that she wasn't up to her elbows in soup making or absorbed in entertaining Joey, her brain had kicked into anxious gear again. She had texted Jackson many times—and called him twice. She received back exactly two texts, neither of any substance, and no returned calls.

Stevie noticed that Marilyn, though an active participant in the conversation, glanced her way from time to time, concern wrinkling her brow. Stevie knew why. Pretty much everyone in their close-knit group had inquired about Jackson in one way or another over the weekend.

"Where's the lad?" Owen had asked.

"What time is Jackson arriving?" Marilyn had inquired, just assuming without question that he would be.

And so on and so on.

Stevie had made cheerful excuses, citing the busyness of the season, to each innocent query, but she knew Marilyn hadn't bought it.

And now, as if sensing her daughter's turn of thoughts, Marilyn reached under the table, took Stevie's hand, and gave it a firm squeeze.

CHAPTER 10

The house was quiet, and Joey was tucked into bed, wiped out from his busy weekend. Syd had retired to his favorite spot in the living room to sleep too —a cushion in front of the little natural gas fireplace. Stevie left the main lights off and sat in the semidarkness, by turns watching the fireplace's orange and yellow flames flicker and then losing herself in the twinkling lights on the room's big Christmas tree.

She stood up when she finally heard Jackson arrive back. With less than a week before Christmas, they both had busy days ahead of them. And like Joey, they were both, no doubt, tired from their weekends too. Every fiber of her being wanted to delay longer, put it off until . . . a better time. But another part of her, the part that had done so much work on herself, knew that nothing good would come of stalling any longer.

Feeling about a hundred years old, she went to meet her husband at the door. And this time, she didn't ask. She told.

"It's time for that talk we keep putting off."

CHAPTER 11

At first, Stevie thought Jackson was going to put her off again, but then he rubbed his hand over his face and massaged his jaw.

"Fine," he said. "Let me grab a shower, at least. I'll meet you in the kitchen."

It felt like Stevie was literally waiting on pins and needles while Jackson showered. She paced the kitchen, doing breathing exercises and trying to calm herself. *You can do this. You can do this,* she chanted in her head while her inner child just cried and cried.

He is going to leave you.

He won't.

He will.

The relentless back and forth was enough to drive her mad. The breathwork wasn't cutting it. She had to get out of her head and back into her body. And there was only one way she knew always worked to do just that.

She turned the oven to 375 degrees to preheat, then went to the fridge and started pulling out ingredients. Inhaling deeply as she peeled fresh garlic and sliced it into generous chunks. Paying attention to the texture of the brie as she scored a very light crosshatch pattern into its top, just through the rind. Noting the give of cheese as she pressed garlic pieces into the slits she'd just made. Concentrating on the feel and scent of fresh thyme as she sprinkled it over the top. A drizzle of truffle oil finished the simple masterpiece. While it baked, she arranged whole pecans, crostini she'd made the day previous, and some dried apricots and cranberries on a platter.

The whole dish from prep to plate took just twenty minutes. Still, it felt like a lifetime had passed by the time Stevie nestled the brie on the platter by the other goodies, and Jackson emerged from the bedroom in a soft navy hoodie and sweats.

He took one of the tall stools near the island. Stevie did the same, pushing the food toward him.

"I thought you might be hungry."

"Thanks," he replied.

Neither of them took a bite, however.

That's okay. It's better to let it rest for a few minutes anyway, Stevie's brain inserted nonsensically.

"So . . . " Jackson said.

"So . . . " Stevie echoed.

Jackson fidgeted. Then he took a pecan, dipped it in the melted cheese, and popped it into his mouth. "Very good," he pronounced.

Stevie nodded and felt herself chickening out. What she—what *they*—had was still so, so much better than so many people. What if she lost it? Lost him?

Her brain piped up again. *Then you had already lost him. It's better to know and to deal with it now than to hold on to a fantasy or imagine love where it doesn't actually exist. You're not a little kid anymore. You don't have to chase love or pretend it's there in order to survive.*

She closed her eyes for half a second, prayed that the right words would come to her, that she'd be heard, not hurt him or herself, and plunged in.

"I love you very, very much," she started, "and this isn't working anymore. I need more. Me and Jackson need more."

Jackson's eyes flashed with anger and defensive indignation. His mouth flew open.

"I want to hear your thoughts. I really do. Please let me finish mine first, though."

Jackson dropped the piece of crostini he'd just picked up and crossed his arms over his chest. Then he nodded.

For the next few minutes, Stevie shared how lonely she was, how she felt like they were growing apart, that there was always too much work. Jackson listened sullenly but without interrupting. And then she asked if he was having an affair with Eloise.

"Are you kidding me?" he exploded. "What kind of man do you think I am?"

"Just answer the question."

"I would never cheat!"

Stevie gave him a long, level look.

"I can't believe you'd even go there."

"No," Stevie said, holding her hands up in a Stop gesture. "This is not me going anywhere. This is me being perfectly fair and minding my own gate. You and Eloise spend a ton of time together, time that you've stopped even mentioning to me. My question isn't unreasonable, and it's not meant as an insult. You and me . . . we're not us anymore. I feel like I've tried everything I know how to do to reach you, and I get nothing back from you. You won't say if you're happy—I feel you're not—but you won't admit if you're mad, sad, whatever you are. All you do is work—"

"Yes! Exactly! All I do is work for you and for our son, and this—" Jackson waved his arm dramatically. "This is what I get? Nagging and questions and endless talk, talk, talk!"

Stevie maintained her kitchen, at home and at work, in a particular way. Everything was tidied up and dealt with every night. The dishes were always done so you could start each day fresh, not mired down by the past's mess. Perishables were properly stored to keep them both safe and to protect their quality and extend their life. The trash was always taken out, so nothing was rotting or stinking up the place. She always aimed to do the same in her relationships with people. Refrain from constantly rehashing the past. You might be passionate, make some messes, or accidentally start some fires, but then you deal with them quickly. Apologize when you've screwed up. Accept others' apologies when they have. Move on. Etcetera. So, this attack cut deeply. She had so determinedly *not* nagged when now she felt like maybe she should have.

She shook her head. "For the past year, I have tried every other means of communication I could think of, from creating elaborate date-night meals to making one-on-one plans that I thought you'd enjoy to suggesting we see a counselor even, or a medical doctor, in case you were depressed."

Jackson's frown deepened to a scowl, and he didn't say he miraculously saw her point or anything. She pushed on. "You seemed to enjoy some of our dates, but just as often, you acted like you were just going through the motions or canceled last minute, just like you did with Christmas decorating the other night."

"Oh, so that's what this is all about. I'm being punished."

Never in her life had Stevie thought a day would come, *could* ever come, that she'd find Jackson unattractive. Apparently, she was wrong. That day had come. Who was this whiny, defensive jerk sitting in front of her?

She ignored his baiting and continued, "You think all counselors are 'quacks,' though, so I saw one by myself for a while, and he was actually very helpful."

It was true. The counselor had been, although one of his comments, "You can't make someone love you," continued to sit painfully with her. She knew it was true.

Jackson was glaring down at the mostly untouched brie dish, not at her. Maybe he wasn't even listening, but she still pressed on.

"You insisted you were not depressed, that you were fine. And as for me wanting to 'talk, talk, talk . . .'" Stevie took a deep breath. "*Of course*, I want that. I want to tell you everything and for you to do the same. We used to talk constantly. We couldn't shut up, in fact. When did that end?"

The last bit was a rhetorical question, but it hurt all the same when Jackson continued to remain silent and didn't even bother to try to respond to her.

"And don't pull any more of that poor me, I work so hard for you and Joey bull," Stevie added, referring to his earlier comment. "You work so hard for *yourself*. I told you I was perfectly happy with our life the way it was. We have more than enough money. I want us to have time together, to play, to dream new dreams, to work to live, not live to work. It's your ego or some issue with your dad or—"

Jackson reared back like Stevie had slapped him. It was a reaction, finally, but not the one she'd been hoping for.

"Don't you dare bring my father up. I'm nothing like him. Nothing."

Stevie shrugged sadly. "If you say so."

"What's that supposed to mean?"

"It's almost inevitable. If we don't revisit our childhoods, try to heal unhealthy patterns, we'll repeat them because they're comfortable, even if we hate them."

Jackson made a scoffing sound. Stevie's eyes welled. She clenched her hands into fists, willing away the tears. "Seriously, when's the last time you played with Joey or read him a bedtime story? Hell, when's the last time you were even *home* before he went to bed?"

Jackson opened his mouth, then shut it. Then he opened it again, keeping his volume low but still somehow managing to sound like he was yelling. "Maybe if you helped out more with the new restaurant, I'd be able to—"

But Stevie wasn't having it. She leaped up from the stool, unable to control the outrage boiling through her. "I told you from Day One I had no interest in a new restaurant right now, that it was more than enough work running the one place, managing staff, etc., etc., while Joey was small. That we were doing more than okay financially, that we didn't need it, wouldn't enjoy it . . . But you insisted, and I got on board! How dare you say differently? I manage practically every detail of the Fox & Hound. I don't even get to cook anymore unless there's a staff shortage. I dress up and smile and take charge of the front of house because you're never there. I haven't even complained about it until now. I've even been excited about it because you were so excited!"

Jackson's head dropped. "You're right. That wasn't fair. I'm sorry."

They were quiet for a moment. The brie had cooled and congealed. Stevie knew that reheating it would salvage it, might even make it better than ever, but for now, it was almost grossly unappetizing.

"I feel like the more I lean in, the more you back away."

Still no response.

Stevie tried a different tack. "How does our marriage, how do *we*, look to you?"

Jackson shrugged and kept his eyes averted, staring at some point beyond her. "We're fine. This is—" He waved his hand, gesturing, Stevie supposed, at the world at large. "Normal marriage stuff."

Stevie bit her lip. "Okay, well . . . text or call me to let me know when you'd like to see Joey over the holidays."

That finally forced Jackson to make eye contact. He shot her an astonished glare, and the blood seemed to drain from his face, giving his light brown skin a slightly greenish cast. "*What?* You're kicking me out?"

"No," Stevie said, sounding calm but feeling anything but. She inhaled for a beat of six seconds, held the breath for six, then let it out in a long stream, counting to eight in her head. "I'm just helping you be more honest and face the choice you already made a while back now, it seems. To leave."

"I don't understand what you want—"

Stevie finally snapped. "That is a lie! You're a smart man. You know exactly what I want. A husband, *my* husband, *you*, to be engaged with me, to be in this with me. To love me." Stevie willed herself not to cry. It seemed to be all she did these days. "I deserve that, Jackson. I have always deserved that."

Jackson swallowed hard, and the belligerence seeped out of him. "So, how does kicking me out help?"

"What's always been our hiring rule at The Fox—your rule initially, but one that immediately clicked for me and that I totally agree to this day is perfect?"

Perhaps it seemed like an abrupt change of subject, but Jackson's grunt of surprise showed he registered her point loud and clear.

Stevie said it aloud, regardless. "The only people we allow in our kitchen are those who genuinely want to be there. Who will do the work because they see the value of it, take joy in it, and want to celebrate the shared reward of it."

He nodded once, his face stony. "Okay, I'll pack a bag."

Somewhere deep inside Stevie, a little kid cried. She wanted to wrap herself around Jackson's legs and beg him not to leave.

Instead, she nodded once. "I'll miss you in my kitchen and at my table," she said and left him to it.

CHAPTER 12

J ackson didn't call or text. Even more strangely, she didn't see him at Fox & Hound either. At some point, she supposed, they'd have to make legal arrangements of some kind, but she couldn't go there—even in her thoughts—right now. It hurt so much that it stole her breath. Gave her heart palpitations. Made her feel constantly on the verge of vomiting. How could she and Jackson be ending? Were they ending? It didn't make sense. They loved each other . . . or she loved him, anyway.

It always baffled Stevie how, when something in your personal life that seemed life-ending occurred, life *didn't* end. It just kept tick-tick-ticking along. She forced herself to go on with daily tasks, however, and everyone was so wrapped up in the season's rush that if she seemed off, they didn't notice.

Mercifully, since returning from the Season of Giving at Cedar Mountain Lodge, there'd been continued staff shortages at Fox & Hound, so between covering shifts Monday and Tuesday and picking up a couple last-minute presents for Joey, she kept herself busy. And Joey, as ever, was in his glory coming to the pub with her. She also made Christmas calls to Alissa and Hailey and was shamefully relieved when she got voicemail. She and Joey left long cheerful messages, which included him singing "We Wish You a Merry Christmas" into her phone. She'd call again after Christmas or early in the New Year and have a real chat. An update. If she had an update. There was that wanna-vomit feeling again.

But she didn't call or reach out to Jackson herself. She couldn't. She was right, and she sensed it deep in her gut. He needed to figure out what he wanted and to act. It was often said that it takes two people to have a failed marriage, but Stevie didn't believe that was true. It took two people to want a marriage to succeed, to last, to work. One person could wreck it perfectly fine on their own if they didn't feel the same as their spouse. If they were *out*. Stevie knew she was far from perfect—but she'd try to fix whatever was making him so unhappy if he'd just do the same. Fight for her. Fight for them. She couldn't save their marriage on her own. She'd already tried and tried . . .

And now it was Wednesday and family Christmas baking day. Stevie wouldn't lie and say her heart wasn't still heavy, but it lifted a little on the drive over to Jo's. Joey had napped, something he didn't usually do, and his sweet little face was pillow-creased. He chattered excitedly from his car seat about the cookies they'd made last year and wondered aloud if they'd make the same ones again. It still blew Stevie away; her son was old enough to have memories. She loved it.

And it would be so good to be surrounded by Maddie, Jo, Lindsey, and the kids. Exactly what her tough, slightly dried-out soul needed: a good basting of love.

She grinned as she pulled into Jo's driveway. Bright Christmassy drawings marked the snowy lawn. Ollie and Grace must've gotten snow markers.

"Joey, look! Santa's on the lawn!"

"Cool!" Joey bounced in his seat excitedly. "Do you think they'll let me try?"

"Maybe, but we might be kept busy with cookies. We'll see."

She parked beside Maddie's car and released Joey from his seat. Aunt Lindsey burst out of the house in a cheerful apron, calling hello to Stevie and picking Joey up to hug him. She proceeded to carry him into the house, much to his delight. Stevie grabbed the container of icing tips and whip bags she'd brought, along with a tote of foodstuff. Jo had insisted she'd buy and organize all the baking ingredients, which was awesome, but Stevie couldn't attend a food-related anything without bringing something.

Maddie rushed over to hug Stevie the second she put her things down in Jo's kitchen. "I'm so glad to see you. It seems like we haven't had time to talk since Thanksgiving."

Stevie stiffened just a little. She didn't want to lie, but this wasn't the time for a serious conversation. "I know. It's been hectic at work and…everything."

Over Maddie's shoulder, Stevie locked eyes with Jo and gave the tiniest shake of her head. Thankfully, Jo understood that she was saying it wasn't the time to broach the topic of her and Jackson's marital issues. She nodded back but looked pensive.

Maddie, nobody's fool, frowned a little as she released Stevie from her embrace. "I think you need some time away to relax. We should book a spa day up at the lodge. Just us girls. Maybe after Christmas?"

"That sounds perfect, Mom."

Jo, Maddie, and Lindsey started chatting about the getaway immediately, but Stevie didn't catch all of it. The details weren't necessary right now—and no doubt would change a few times before it all got settled. And anyway, where or what they did wasn't important. She was just happy to have them in her life.

Her eyes misted, and she smiled at her family. "You guys are the best. You really are."

"We know, we know," Jo joked, and Stevie could've kissed her for lifting the mood and steering the conversation away from her. "Now, let's get at it. These cookies aren't going to bake themselves!"

The rest of the afternoon and evening passed in a cookie-scented haze of light conversation, laughter, the happy surprise that Lindsey was moving from Boise to live in Granite Ridge permanently—and the news that she had a hot date at the Fox & Hound on the twenty-third. She sounded excited and nervous, which made them all tease her happily. Well, all except Stevie. She was happy for her aunt but not in the mood to be boisterous.

There was also much, much snacking and so, so many cookies. Stevie lost count of how many they made and decorated and felt almost beside herself with gratitude. The busyness and the warmth of her family almost—almost—kept thoughts of Jackson at bay, and even when they did sneak in, having so much love around her was a comfort and a reminder. Whatever happened, however heartbreaking it might be, she and Joey would be just fine.

They would, wouldn't they?

Stevie believed it, she did—but still, at the end of the night, when Jo gave her a hug goodbye after she loaded Joey and all their cookies into the van, it was all she could do to not break down.

"Let me know if there's anything I can do to help you guys. *Anything*," Jo said a little ferociously.

Stevie nodded and wiped her nose, feeling like a kid.

"And if things don't change or something better doesn't

come up, you and Joey come here for dinner on the twenty-fourth. Promise."

Stevie promised.

CHAPTER 13

The twenty-third dawned—if you could call the sludge-gray "dawn"—and still no call or word from Jackson.

Stevie made fresh fruit salad cups, basted eggs on sourdough, and grilled asparagus for her and Joey for breakfast. As she cooked, she faced the fact that even though she thought she'd been resolved about what drawing a line might mean for her marriage, some deep inner part of her was . . . shellshocked. She'd naively been sure there was something to salvage. That there was love on both sides, but apparently not. *Where was he?*

She tried to distract herself with practical concerns, like the fridge full of fresh food she'd ordered for Christmas week, back when she thought the three of them would be enjoying a holiday at home during Fox & Hound's shutdown from December 24th through the 30th. When she'd envisioned family and friends popping by for festive visits and merry eats.

She felt sick. What had she done? What had she done?

The only thing you could, dear, brave girl. The only thing you could. Stevie wasn't sure if it was Maddie or Marilyn's voice that spoke in her head, but it helped get her back on track—as did Joey's voice calling from the table, "If you don't come and get it, I'm going to eat it allllll."

His giggle showed he was joking—and copying what Stevie often said to tease him and Jackson when she had meals ready.

"No, wait! Save some for me," she called back, echoing what Joey always said when he'd come running.

It didn't miss her notice, either, that Joey hadn't even asked where Jackson was. That, even more than Maddie and Marilyn's assurance in her head, affirmed Stevie's gut that as painful as it might be, things had come to this point . . . That Joey didn't even register Jackson's multiple days and nights' absence as worthy of comment showed how absent he'd been, not just from Stevie's days but from his son's.

"Can we bring all my stuffies and put them around the Christmas tree and sing 'Rock Around the Christmas Tree?' It's like 'Rock Around the Clock,' but with Christmas!"

Stevie burst out laughing. How could she not? What a comfort a little person was. "We absolutely can. Absolutely! Go grab them."

She made a mental note to tell Hailey about this song modification, knowing she and her musician husband, Nick, would get an extreme kick out of it. And she'd have to tell Gramma and Gramps too. It was undoubtedly Marilyn who'd introduced Joey to the 1956 hit. She loved old rock and roll and anything vintage second only to her love for Jamie, sweets—and her daughter and grandson.

Joey had a Christmas party at a school friend's that evening—a fact that made Stevie's head spin a little. If it was a family gig, she'd get it, but your own Christmas party when you were six? Mind-boggling! Even after tidying and cleaning the already tidy and clean house and rocking around the Christmas tree many, many times, there was a lot of time to fill before then.

To keep herself from going crazy with questions, Stevie took Joey sledding at one of the nearby parks that had long, gentle slopes. Inez and Ana were both there with their charges, and the kids had a great time, going up and down the hill again and again while the women chatted.

"Thanks for giving Callie the promotion. She's very happy," Inez said at one point in the conversation.

"I'm the one who's happy! She's fantastic, and she couldn't have hired on at a better time," Stevie said, meaning every word of her praise.

As if cued by reference to the pub, the tinkling notes of "Wish Upon A Star" filled the air—the ringtone Stevie had set for the Fox & Hound.

She pulled it out of her pocket. "Hello? Stevie here."

Three minutes of panic ensued. The chef was—again—unable to make it in. They'd tried calling Jackson, but he didn't pick up. Stevie bit her lip, thinking. Should she be *worried* about Jackson? It was one thing to ditch her. It was another to ditch the pub—

Focus, Fox!

"Give me a second or two. I'll call you back."

"Do you need to work?" Ana asked as Stevie ended the call.

"Yes, that would be ideal, but Joey has that party at—"

"Amber's home, yes. Our kids are going too. I could watch Joey for you. It goes surprisingly late—till nine o'clock."

Stevie thought about it. The Fox & Hound switched from offering a full dinner menu to more basic pub fare at 8:30. Callie was on, and the other sous chef was good too. If she joined them for the main dinner service, all would be fine.

"Would Zachary's parents mind you doing double duty, chaperoning my kid while watching theirs?"

Ana shook her head decisively. "They'll be fine with it, I'm sure, but I'll check." She whipped out her phone, and her thumbs flew. She'd barely hit send when the answer came back. She scanned the reply and grinned. "You're all set."

"Wow, thank you much!"

Joey was thrilled to get to play at Zachary's house before the party, and per usual, Stevie was struck by how different her son's childhood was from her own. Except now he was going to be raised by a single mom too. She closed her eyes for the briefest second. She had the best possible role models of how—and how not to—do that. She'd be fine. Her extended family would help her. She wasn't like Marilyn had been. She wasn't alone.

"Are you okay?" Inez asked softly.

Stevie flinched. That question again. "I'm fine—or I will be. Just some complicated stuff going on."

Inez nodded. "That sounds about right. All the great, good, and bad mixed up together. Makes decisions hard."

The comment was so on the nose that Stevie was a bit startled. "Are you clairvoyant?"

Inez laughed. "No, it's just always true about life."

Stevie couldn't argue with that.

The shift passed quickly, and Stevie enjoyed every minute of it. She loved being in her chef blacks and just cooking, but the servers must've told patrons that she was in the kitchen. There were several requests for her to pop out for a visit if she had a chance. This kind of greet-your-eaters thing was more Jackson's cup of tea than hers, and he was so good at it—

Stop it! she commanded herself. *You are just fine at it too.* And she was. When the dinner service started to wind down and the music volume went up, she went around visiting tables, asking how everything was, thanking them for coming in, and wishing people a Merry Christmas.

It was the first year she'd done the Christmas greetings solo. Usually, it was her and Jackson together, united.

"You two, just so sweet," some older woman inevitably gushed. She pushed thoughts of how much stronger and social she felt with charismatic Jackson by her side and focused instead on what she did best. The food. There hadn't been a single complaint—rare in service, no matter how well a night went, but she'd take it. People commented especially positively on the seasonal specials, both the squash risotto and the rosemary and garlic studded slow-roasted lamb, getting rave reviews.

She smiled as she neared the booths by the streetside of the pub and saw Marilyn in animated conversation with Jamie, who was smiling down at his petite wife with such open affection that Stevie's throat clogged. She was so, so happy for her mother. If anyone had deserved a break, it was her.

"Hi, Mom. Hi, Jamie."

Marilyn whirled around in her seat, beaming from ear to ear. "Sweetie! I hoped we'd see you tonight. You outdid yourself with the menu this year."

"You say that every year."

"And she's always right," Jamie said. "That lamb." He pinched his forefinger and thumb together and kissed them to show how delicious he'd found it. "Tres Magnifique!" His Irish-accented French was hilarious, and Stevie laughed.

"And you," she said, directing her comment to her mother. "I know you didn't eat lamb."

Marilyn shuddered. "Of course not."

"Let me guess, you went straight for the sugar packets?"

"Ha ha," Marilyn said, smiling beatifically. "But close. You know me well."

"She did not!" Stevie said with feigned horror that was not quite feigned.

"She did," Jamie nodded with mock sad solemnity.

"I should've known when that came up as a special request. Who else would order Candy Mountain Madness as *dinner?*"

"It's very hearty," Marilyn said in a prim voice, but her eyes sparkled.

"Oh, yes—a stack of pancakes with alternating layers of chocolate sauce, melted peanut butter, sliced bananas, and whipping cream. All topped off with assorted gummy candies. Very *hearty*," Stevie mocked gently, her voice soft with fondness. The dessert-meal was special to her too, which was why it was on the menu in the first place. Marilyn had invented it in honor of Stevie on her ninth birthday.

"Also, it's a double tradition. You and I made it together when you were little, and it's what I ate on our first date." Marilyn smiled up at Jamie.

Stevie would've said *Gross*, but to quote one of the older women she'd just been thinking about, they really were "sooo sweet," so she couldn't.

Instead, she rolled her eyes. "It's utterly mad."

"Yeah, mad-delicous!" Marilyn said, giggling like Joey. Stevie suddenly wanted to hug her, so she did.

"Aw, sweetie. Thank you," Marilyn said, hugging back and sounding pleased.

Stevie was about to ask them what time they were heading up to Cedar Mountain Lodge, where they went every year to celebrate their anniversary, but Marilyn's phone buzzed with a text.

Whatever Marilyn read pinched her face with worry. "I'm

sorry. I have to make a phone call." She got up and practically ran from the table.

Stevie and Jamie exchanged a look, but he just shrugged, and his concerned gaze followed his wife.

"Should I go after her?"

"No, no," Jamie said. "You're busy. I've got her."

He always did. It was true. Stevie smiled wistfully. "Okay, well, tell her Merry Christmas for me—I'm sure me and Joey will make it to see you guys at the lodge for at least one day."

Jamie looked even more confused, but Stevie suddenly realized she desperately needed to pee. She got so used to holding it when she was in the kitchen that sometimes she forgot until it was urgent.

"Merry Christmas! Talk soon."

"Okay, yeah," Jamie called to her departing back.

Stevie pushed open the bathroom door and stopped in her tracks. Lindsey was there, sans Maddie, which was always weird for Stevie. She was used to them being practically inseparable. Then, a tidbit of conversation from the family baking day came back to her that she hadn't really had much heart for at the time. Right! Lindsey had a date with some handsome man or unrequited love or something tonight.

She forced enthusiasm into her voice because Lord knew it wasn't her aunt's fault romance wasn't high on Stevie's list of favorite things this Christmas. "Hey, Linds! How's the date going?"

To her surprise—and almost horror—Lindsey turned a blotchy red and seemed on the verge of tears upon seeing her. "You've gotta get me out here. Please, Stevie. I can't breathe. I need fresh air. I can't go back out there. I can't see him. Is there a back door? A way out that won't take me past the dining room?"

Stevie was startled but quickly jumped into action. "Sure. Follow me."

She led Lindsey to a door that said *Staff Only* and then took her through the kitchen and out the back door.

"What's wrong?" Stevie asked once they were outside. "Are you all right?"

"No. Yes. I don't know. Crap! I don't have my car. Does Granite Ridge have cabs? Or Uber?"

"We have both. What happened? Are you okay?"

"He's married."

"*What?*"

"Armando's married. I overheard someone ask him about his wife, and he confirmed it."

Stevie saw red. What was with all these rotten men anyway? "That jerk! You've gotta be kidding me."

"I wish I was." Lindsey shivered and wrapped her arms more tightly around her waist. "I definitely didn't see that coming. Not from Mondo. He was my best friend. I thought I could trust him."

Stevie was at a loss for what to say. She wished Maddie or Jo or even Marilyn was there—someone, anyone, more equipped to give relationship advice than she was. She rubbed her aunt's arm. "I'm so sorry. That sucks so hard. I wish I could think of something more profound to say, but it just…sucks. There's no other way to put it."

Lindsey looked away from Stevie. "I can't believe this. After all this time…"

A brisk wind kicked up just then, but when Lindsey shivered again, Stevie felt it was from sorrow, shock, and betrayal more than the cold. And how she related. White hot anger sparked deep inside her. She'd been telling herself she only felt sad about Jackson, but that wasn't entirely true. She'd learned to manage her temper over the past years and had done a lot of work to recognize that anger was just the easiest go-to emotion for her—that often, what she first interpreted as anger was possibly sorrow or fear or some other uncomfortable feeling. But right now? Her anger was not misinterpreted anything. Nope, it was good old-fashioned fury. These men!

The wind kicked up with a vengeance that matched the one Stevie felt like handing out.

"Where's your coat?" she asked Lindsey.

"I left it at my seat." Lindsey groaned. "I was on my way back from the restroom when I overheard a conversation and learned he has a wife waiting at home. I just ran away. I didn't go back to the table."

"So, he doesn't know you know?"

Lindsey shook her head. "No. I'll confront him at some point, but not right now. Not while it feels so raw."

"I understand. Why don't you wait inside where it's warm? I'll grab your coat from that louse and call you a cab."

"I don't need the coat. I have others. And I can call a cab or book a rideshare with my phone. I know you're busy. You need to get back to work. Sorry you got caught up in my drama."

"Hey, no, don't worry about me. I'm glad I was able to be here. We're family. We look out for each other. Which is why I don't feel comfortable just leaving you out here in the cold. Why don't you wait in the kitchen while I call a cab? And you shouldn't have to give up your coat. I'm happy to get it for you."

"What would you tell him?"

"I don't know." Stevie knew it was a lie, even as she shrugged nonchalantly. "I'd probably say that you don't feel well and that you need to head home. And then I might suggest he head home too . . . to his wife." *And I might say it a lot more strongly than that, creep face.*

Lindsey winced. "That's okay. I don't want to cause any

scenes in your restaurant. Thank you, though. It means a lot to know you care. I'll be fine. Really. It was just a shock. That's all."

Stevie shot a glance over her shoulder. A cab wasn't right for this situation. Maybe she could snag Marilyn and Jamie— but then she thought better of that too. It was Maddie she should call. Definitely. Lindsey needed Maddie whether she felt comfortable asking for the help or not.

"I'm fine," Lindsey insisted again. "I promise. You head back inside. I'm gonna walk a little ways down the street, so I'm not waiting for my ride out front in case Armando comes out looking for me."

"At least let me call you a ride. Please? There's a bar open around the corner, two doors down. I'll arrange for you to be picked up there so you can wait inside."

"All right." Lindsey nodded. "Thanks, Stevie."

Stevie remembered when she used to be uncomfortable with hugs or physical displays of affection. That was a long time ago now, and she was so glad she'd overcome it because sometimes a hug was the only comfort you could offer. She wrapped her arms around Lindsey and squeezed her hard. Then she strode off on a mission, dialing Maddie and getting her en route before heading into the Fox & Hound.

Armando Valdivieso was sitting at one of their most private tables. Tosser. He *was* handsome. Douche bag. He was sipping water. Stevie couldn't think of an insult to go with that.

Their server Neil was approaching with plates—what timing.

"Ah, Neil. Perfect timing!"

Neil smiled but looked a little confused. Fair.

"There's been a change of plans for Mr. Valdivieso—oh, I'm sorry. I mean for *Mondo*," Stevie said snidely. "Can you box his food up for him very, very quickly?"

"What? Pardon? I don't understand," Armando said, sounding genuine—which made Stevie want to punch him. If he was this good an actor, no wonder Lindsey fell for it.

Neil quickly and smoothly disappeared to do as asked, and Stevie took that opportunity to whisk Lindsey's coat from the back of her empty chair.

Armando jumped to his feet, almost protectively, which was such a joke.

"Hey, that's my—"

"Your *what*? Your mistress's coat? Your sidepiece's jacket?"

"What? No!" Armando was good—or rather, really, really awful. He seemed truly horrified by her insinuations.

"That's right, *no*. My Aunt Lindsey is worth a thousand of you—and she's nobody's trashy affair. Don't contact her again." Stevie said all this very bitingly but in a low voice and with a smile. No nearby tables would be wise to what was going on.

Neil reappeared with a stuffed bag of food at record speed. Nice! Stevie took it from him, thanked him sincerely, and passed the bag to Armando. "It's on me. Your money's no good here. Now take this and get out. Go eat it with your *wife*."

Armando took the bag of food that Stevie practically shoved at him.

"But—"

Stevie put her hands on her hips and raised an eyebrow.

Whatever excuse Armando was going to try to give, he apparently thought better of. He didn't bother to put on his own coat. Just grabbed it with his free hand and skedaddled out of the pub.

Skedaddled. Eloise's word. Ugh. It wasn't lost on Stevie that her anger, while definitely meant for Valdivieso, was also targeted at Jackson. And possibly Eloise. Maybe they were together at this moment? Stevie had thought there was *danger* of an affair, not that they'd already started one. Maybe she was wrong?

She sighed heavily. Well, she'd had about five hours of not thinking obsessively about her marriage issues. That was something.

She went and said goodbye to her staff, finding them each one by one to wish them a Merry Christmas and to remind them they'd do a staff party in January. She smiled happily to herself, knowing they'd each receive a merry little Christmas surprise bonus before then too. It was important to her and Jackson—*sigh*—that the staff benefit from all their hard work and the Fox & Hound's success too. Then she went to pick up Joey from his party.

Two more sleeps till Christmas. She'd never in her life, or not since being taken in by Maddie anyway, imagined that she'd ever dread Christmas, yet here she was . . .

CHAPTER 14

Stevie stirred and stretched out in her warm sheets beneath the down duvet. It was so, so nice to wake naturally, without an alarm blaring—

A different alarm blared, making her bolt upright, heart racing: reality.

She was in bed *alone*. Stretched out *alone*. It was Christmas Eve, and Jackson still wasn't home. She pressed her hand hard against her sternum and did a series of breathing exercises until her anxiety eased. Then she rubbed her eyes, which felt grainy and puffy after all the crying she'd done last night after Joey went to sleep.

All the delicious, easy forgetfulness that sleep had granted her was obliterated. Stevie got up, pulled her robe on, and quickly let Syd out the back to do his business. Then she headed to the shower. She wanted to make sure she looked as fresh and peaceful as possible when Joey woke up.

She didn't get very far. Her hand was on the door to the washroom when she heard the front door opening—or thought she did. She froze and listened hard. Was she just delusional?

No. It was definitely the door.

Stevie padded softly down the hall, staying close to the wall, out of the door's immediate line of sight. She paused by the entrance to the kitchen, then detoured and grabbed her heavy marble rolling pin from where it hung in brackets on the wall. Then she exited the kitchen by its other door that opened into the front entrance, aiming to surprise the intruder.

She succeeded because when she saw who it was, she dropped the marble rolling pin in shock. It clanked loudly against the stone tile.

Jackson, his back to her as he pushed one snowy shoe off with the toe of his other, jumped. Then almost stumbled. He wheeled around.

"Stevie."

She stared at him. Finally found words. They came out in a pained wheeze like the dying whistle of a teakettle taken off the burner. "What are *you* doing here?"

He bit his lip. Stevie noticed he had a fresh haircut, buzzed short above his ears, with more length—those curls— on the top. He was freshly shaven too. And his shirt was crisp. He was obviously doing well. While she was—

She looked down. In her favorite, most ratty old bathrobe with a hole in one armpit that nearly revealed her breast. With her face a blotchy, swollen, telltale mess of misery, no doubt. Her stupid milk-pale skin never let her hide her emotions. But this glaring contrast between the two of them was for the best. Things had never seemed so clear to her. One of these things was not like the other. One of these things does not belong.

That's your trauma talking.

That doesn't mean it isn't true.

Jackson stared at her. She stared at him.

"I asked *what* are you doing here?" she repeated. Rage was

stirring in her belly in a way it hadn't in years. A slurry of sadness and fear thickened her voice to a growl. "You do not get to disappear and go no contact for a whole week, then waltz back into the house unannounced like everything's A-OK. If it wasn't Christmas, the locks would already be changed."

Jackson winced. "I . . . I wanted to surprise you."

"Well, you succeeded. Now get out. You can call me in the new year, and we'll figure out the mess. Not now. Not at"—to Stevie's great irritation, she got choked up on the last word—"Christmas."

Jackson pinned his gaze to the floor. "Shoot, shoot, shoot," he whispered. "Marilyn was right."

"Marilyn!" Stevie practically screeched—then fought to lower her voice so Joey wouldn't be woken up. "What does my mother have to do with any of this? Wait a minute, wait a minute, wait a minute—" Stevie stuttered as her brain flashed on her encounter with Marilyn at the Fox & Hound the night before. "Did you text her? Did she know you'd left me, left *us*?"

The extra sense of betrayal was too much. Stevie sank to the floor beside the stupid, useless rolling pin and wrapped her arms around herself. Marilyn had known and not said a word, not reached out, not done anything to help her? She'd sided in silence with Jackson for some reason?

"No, no, no—this is all wrong. I got this—I did this—all wrong." Jackson sounded as broken as Stevie felt, and it gave her pause. He lowered himself to the floor beside her.

"Please let me try to explain." He reached for her hand.

Stevie shifted away and didn't let him touch her. "Explain what? That we're done. That you don't love me anymore? It's okay. I get it. I don't want some big dramatic conversation about it."

"Aw, Stevie. No. It's the opposite of what you think. I'm just . . . Marilyn was right."

"Stop bringing up Marilyn!" Her brain was screaming inside. The triggers were too much. *Too much.* She'd done a lot of work. She'd forgiven her Marilyn. She truly had. Her biological mother had done the best she could at the time, but Stevie couldn't bear sitting here, her marriage falling apart, her husband leaving her, and having it turn out that the mom she'd longed for and longed for as a kid, who had abandoned her over and over, was somehow a participant in this betrayal.

The triggers are not too much. You can deeply, deeply hurt, and *you can be okay. You can go through extremely painful, difficult things,* and *you can go on and find good things again.*

"Okay, Jackson. No more poor you, I screwed up mystery-as-to-what-you're-actually-trying to say. Spill. Now. Please! I'm really, really confused, but I'm listening."

"Thank you." As if Jackson had borrowed a page out of one of her books, he took a deep breath, paused, then exhaled. "Marilyn didn't know anything, not until yesterday —and even then, not much. I borrowed a couple books from her early in the week. Then yesterday, I called her to arrange childcare, and she realized I wasn't staying at the house—and well, she kind of freaked out."

Jackson had borrowed books from Marilyn? Stevie didn't ask about it because he was already pushing on.

"I tried to calm her down by telling her about my plan to surprise you, but she told me it was a terrible idea—that you'd feel like I had abandoned you."

"She should've said I would feel like you abandoned me because you *did* abandon me."

Jackson hung his head.

"What were you doing? You didn't call? You couldn't text?" Stevie had so many other, more significant questions, but those were the ones that blurted out. Why did he need childcare, for example? She was the one who arranged all that, for crying out loud—and he needed to come to her for decisions regarding Joey visits, not Marilyn. And another thing—

"I spent the first two days just being . . . angry," Jackson admitted.

Try to listen to him. To really hear him without planning what you want to say in response while he's talking. You'll get your chance. Stevie wanted to slap her inner voice in its know-it-all face, but she also knew it was good advice.

"Go on."

"And then I realized that you were just . . . absolutely right about everything."

A startled yelp of a laugh escaped Stevie. She shook her head. "I'm not following at all. I don't understand."

Jackson laughed a little too. "It's convoluted. I don't blame you. I'll try to give you a rough outline. I read one of the books that Marilyn gave you that you were always wanting me to read too."

"Which one?"

"The one on attachment or whatever that I thought was so trendy and just the newest psychobabble." He smiled to show he knew he was quoting himself and had changed his opinion. He reached for her hand again. This time, Stevie let him take it.

The slide of his skin against hers, the comfortable sensation of their fit as he linked his fingers through hers, made her inhale sharply. No breathing exercise this time. Longing, pure and simple. Terrified hope. Was he not . . . leaving?

He must've read her expression. "I am an idiot, and I hate that I hurt you and made you feel insecure. I hate it more than you will ever, ever know, but angry as I was, I never planned to leave you. It didn't even enter my mind. I was already focusing on how to win you back. It just didn't occur to me what you would see my lack of contact as."

"Then you really, really are an idiot," she said.

He nodded, and his eyes crinkled, but just a little. They weren't out of the woods yet, and he seemed to know it too. Just as quickly as hope had flared in Stevie, it was doused by a new thought.

"Eloise," she said simply. "I just don't know if I can forgive—"

"Me being a fool? I hope you can. Me being a cheater? You never should. I swear I did not have an affair of any kind with Eloise. It's another thing that truly never entered my mind."

Stevie scoffed.

"For real, Stevie. It was all about the new pub for me. That's it. I got a bit . . . obsessed."

"To put it mildly."

"Yeah." He looked pained, though he tried to smile. "That's fair. But when I got over being offended by you, I totally could see where you were coming from and why you were worried. And I'm sorry. You can talk to her if you want."

Stevie shook her head and studied her husband's face. She'd known Jackson since they were teenagers. She would've sworn she could tell if he was lying, but now . . . now she didn't know.

"You're telling me you guys never discussed having any kind of feelings for each other or entertained any what if you weren't married conversations?"

Jackson looked like he might cry, something Stevie had never seen him do. "Never."

"And you never touched her or kissed her or tried to— and she never touched you or kissed you?" Just having to ask, having to have it spelled out, made her ill.

"No, Stevie." Jackson's voice cracked. "*No*."

She looked down at their hands, still linked, resting on his thigh, then into his eyes.

"There was a time when I probably was the kind of woman who would've played the 'Pick me, pick me' game. Who would've been frantic to hold on to what I thought I had in you at all costs. Who, so sure it was some failing in me, some flaw, some lack, that I would've abandoned myself just to try to keep you. But I am not that sad, broken little kid who thinks, who truly believes, that no one will ever love me as much as I love them. Not anymore."

She inhaled. A line she'd read somewhere about relationships came back to her. Something about how you should never have to explain to your person what your value is or why you're valuable. If they don't already see your worth and know your value, you'll never convince them. You'll only do the opposite trying. Stevie could see truth in that, but she wasn't saying what she was about to say for him. She was saying it for herself. To herself. To remind her of what adult Stevie knew was true, even if she didn't always feel it.

"I'm a frigging catch, Jackson. I'm loyal to my bones. I'm tough and hardworking. I'm clueless and loud sometimes, but I'm also kind. I clean up okay. Sometimes I'm funny—"

Stevie became aware of tears sliding down her cheeks only when Jackson reached out to wipe one away. "You are more than a catch, Stevie Fox," he said gruffly. "And you are all those things you said and way, way more."

He tried to gently pull her into an embrace, but she wasn't done yet.

"I can love you—*and* I can let you go if we're toxic together. You are either with me, pouring into me what I pour into you, or you're out."

Jackson nodded. "I hear what you're saying, and I know you're right. That's why I got—why I am—so afraid."

"*You're* afraid. Of what?"

"You. You're so strong, so smart, so fearless."

Stevie shook her head. "Nope. Super needy. Vulnerable. Always scared."

"Nah. You might feel those things, but you always push through, keep learning, keep growing. . . You're amazing, and I get worried you'll outgrow me. Realize I'm just a boring guy. I wanted to get Two off the ground as a way of showing you—I don't even know. When I say it out loud, it's stupid."

"Yeah, it is," Stevie said, feeling all sorts of things that had been tied too tightly for too long loosen and unknot. "We're both really ef—messed up, hey?"

He nodded and pulled her close. This time, she didn't resist.

"I know this doesn't totally . . . fix everything between us yet," he said, his chin resting on the top of her head. "I know I still have some amends to make. And I know we'll have to have some more tough conversations."

Stevie didn't agree or disagree. She just waited.

She felt his lips against her hair, and he whispered, "I'm sorry about that too."

"About what?"

"When I got all bent of shape because you didn't want me to mess up your hair."

"It's okay. Really."

"No, it's not," Jackson insisted. "I get it now. Eloise explained it to me actually—and she called me a cad."

It still rankled that Jackson had talked to Eloise about her, about their relationship. Also, it showed he had been in a danger zone, whether he'd admit it to himself or not. That was intimate talk.

"And trust me, when she says 'cad,' it sounds very, very bad."

That made Stevie laugh just a little, and curiosity got the best of her. "And just what exactly did *Eloise* explain?"

"That if a man's hair gets messed up, it's a two-minute fix. For a woman with a beautiful mane like yours, it's a lot more."

"She's not wrong."

"And I know primping and preening isn't your favorite thing, but you do it because of the role you took on—for me. It was disrespectful, and I'm sorry."

Stevie craned her head to look up at him. "Just so long as you know that unless I'm going to work or an event, I am really, really happy for you to mess up my hair."

Jackson grinned and made a contented sound. "Yeah, I count on it."

Stevie crinkled her nose. She really, really wanted to resist but couldn't. "Was that all Eloise told you when she called you a cad?"

"No," Jackson said ruefully. "And the hair thing wasn't even the reason. Her exact words were, 'Get your head out of your derriere, Jackson, you cad, and don't bring up you and your wife's business to me again. If you have issues with your relationship, tell her, not me. It's not appropriate, and I don't want to hear it.'"

"She's not wrong," Stevie said, repeating her earlier comment. Then she smiled so wide she felt it in her cheekbones. "I always knew I liked her."

And Stevie wasn't lying. She had liked Eloise, and now her respect for her had deepened. Too many women had no qualms about husband poaching. She saw leaches like that all the time at the pub.

"I'm glad," Jackson continued, "because she isn't an issue. I didn't—and will never—be unfaithful to you in the way you feared. And I'll work on being faithful in maintaining your and my connection from here on out, always too. Ditto with Marilyn. She wasn't in on anything behind your back. I was trying to arrange childcare. For the surprise."

Oh right. That whole tangent. Stevie had totally forgotten.

"I want to take you and Joey to Cedar Mountain Lodge for Christmas. We can have time together as a family, but you and I can steal some alone time too. Marilyn said she and Jamie would be 'delighted' to spend some of their anniversary week with Joey."

"I'll bet she did," Stevie said, smiling. "But how on earth did you get us a room? Aren't they booked solid? Did you get Robert to pull some strings—"

An ecstatic squeal cut her off. "Dad! Dad! I knew you wouldn't be too busy or forget me or Christmas. I knew it!"

Stevie and Jackson were stunned to silence for a second, and Jackson's grip on her hand tightened. He was obviously hit by the same realization she was. Their little son hadn't been as oblivious—or as fine with—his Daddy's absence as Stevie had hoped he was. Which made sense. Kids saw everything and understood things adults always wished they wouldn't.

But it's never too late to do better, her inner voice said softly. *Yeah, yeah,* her other inner self sniped back—but she did feel grateful. It was true.

"Of course, you're right, sweetie! Dad would never be too busy for Christmas, and he would never, ever forget you," she said.

"I knew it," Joey said, half boastingly, half nonchalantly. He shrugged. "It's because he loves you and me more than anything in the universe, not just to the moon and back."

Oh, thank God, Stevie thought. It wasn't a cuss. It was a prayer. Their nonsense hadn't jeopardized Joey's certainty of his position in their hearts. He'd clearly had unvoiced questions, but it wasn't dire. Out loud she said, "That's a whole lot of love, all right."

"Yeah," Joey said with satisfaction.

"It really is," Jackson whispered against Stevie's hair, then kissed her neck just below her ear. Her heart swelled with hope. Please let them really, truly be repaired. Please.

CHAPTER 15

The drive up to Cedar Mountain Lodge with Jackson and Joey was . . . weird. The trip itself was gorgeous as always, with all the mountains and trees blanketed in white and a soft dance of swirling snow. But Stevie felt, of all things, self-conscious. It was like she and Jackson were on best behavior or something. Not that being polite and careful was bad, but it felt awkward. Like they'd moved from being lovers and the closest of friends to very conscientious, wanting to please strangers. She wanted their old ease and chemistry back.

Thankfully, Joey was in a hyper mood, fueled no doubt by the sugar cookies he was happily demolishing out of a plastic tote of the ones they'd made on family baking day. Eventually, his wanting to sing carols and tell silly Christmas jokes —apparently, Amber's party had featured a joke-telling Santa Clown—wore off on them, and the tension eased.

As Jackson turned into the huge parking area, Stevie couldn't help gawking. She had high hopes for their week together, and the scenery apparently got her mental memo. It surpassed its usual magic. So beautiful it made her heart ache: the now familiar-as-friends towering cedars. The purple sky. The ancient mountain ranges, so protective and majestic. The picturesque ski village lit up with a dazzling array—

"Happy to be here?" Jackson asked, his eyes twinkling like the lights.

"Yes!" Joey cheered.

Stevie was about to agree, but then she noticed Jackson had turned the wrong way. He was following the signs toward a designated area for overnight parking. She pointed in the opposite direction from the one they were headed. "You're going the wrong way."

Jackson cocked an eyebrow in that slightly sexy way he had. "Am I?"

Confused and about to reply, *Yes, you are*, the words caught in Stevie's throat. She could only stare in disbelief.

"No way." She shot Jackson an incredulous look, then immediately redirected her gaze to what she still wasn't sure she believed she was seeing.

"Way," Jackson said, using the corny 90s slang and nodding.

"The RV? You got it out and brought it all the way up here? Are you kidding me?"

"It was a huge ordeal. It was parked behind three of my dad's cars in the garage," Jackson said, but he was only feigning the complaints. His tone showed he was already thrilled by her response.

Stevie clasped her hands together in her lap and rocked lightly back and forth. "Aw, it's perfect, Jackson. Just perfect!"

And it really was.

Memories of her and Jackson's first Christmas flooded back, the one where they'd reconnected during Alissa's tumultuous wedding week. How they'd ridden out a huge storm together. Where they'd gotten married. *Online*. She giggled.

"I don't get. Why is Mom laughing? What's so funny?" Joey asked. "Is that our motorhome? Are we going to camp in the *snow?*"

"I think Mom's just happy, big guy—and yes, camping in the snow is great. You'll see."

"I thought we'd have a room with a jacuzzi."

"Oh my," said Jackson.

Stevie finally tore her gaze away from her vintage 1986 Toyota Sunrader, so darling with the strings of colored bulbs Jackson had meticulously outlined it with. They glowed merrily through a light dusting of snow.

"Thank you," she said softly.

"Just wait," he said, matching her tone. "You ain't seen nothing yet."

He parked in front of the RV and helped Joey out of his seatbelt, then stuffed him into his boots and coat while Stevie put Syd's leash on him. She was so happy she'd brought his blue sequined collar and leash. This place—and the RV—had been where she first got him too. It was only appropriate he was also wearing his best duds from that Christmas.

Jackson had thought of everything. Not just the exterior Christmas lights were set up, but the RV was plugged in, and the stove, heater, and pump were ready to go. And he'd decorated it similarly to how she had all those years ago—minus her special ornament collection because that, of course, decorated the tree in their shared home now.

Her wee little pre-wired tree sat on the wide shelf above the kitchen counter, and Jackson had anchored it in place with the tie-down system Stevie had come up with. The tree's warm white lights danced and dimmed in various patterns set with a small remote, getting brighter or more twinkly, then fading away and starting again. Jackson had even remembered the swath of purple satin she used in lieu of a tree skirt and had wrapped the fabric around the base of the tree in a loose flourish that hid the base and tie-downs.

A string of lights hung across the back window of the RV in a soft scallop shape too, just the way she'd arranged them back in the day, with a small wreath in the center.

Stevie shook her head. "I can't believe you did this, that you pulled it all off . . ." She opened the fridge and was impressed. Her stomach growled, which made Jackson laugh.

"See, I really do still know the way to your heart."

"Absolutely."

It was a small space for a dog, two grown-ups, and a Christmas-hyper Joey, who was peeking into cupboards and checking out the small freezer that doubled as a counter.

"Did you remember the chocolate-covered cherries and the potstickers?" he asked, almost in a panic.

"Yes, I did—and wow, are you ever your mother's son!"

Joey's brow furrowed. "Of course I am. That doesn't even make sense."

Stevie and Jackson laughed, and Stevie noted it was the second time in short succession that Joey said something his parents said didn't make sense. *Get used to it, little man*, she thought.

"So I was thinking . . . " Jackson said, sounding almost shy, which Stevie found beyond adorable. "Maybe the three of us could have some lunch, and then maybe Joey could go hang out with Marilyn and Jamie—they said their schedule is wide open—and you and I could have a little nap?"

"A little nap, hey?" Stevie teased, a light simmering heat starting low in her belly. "That's what we're calling it now?"

"Gramma and Gramps! Gramma and Gramps!" chanted Joey in rhythm with his jumping on the bed. "I don't want a nap. I hate naps!"

"Oh, you'll like them one day, Joey, I promise," Jackson said, wrapping his arms around Stevie from behind.

Joey stopped jumping. "You can nap, but first you said you'd feed me and Mom."

Stevie laughed so hard she almost couldn't stop. It wasn't that the comment was *that* funny; it was just that she had this crazy upwelling of joy. These were the moments she treasured most with her family, these silly, would-totally-be-forgotten everyday moments of togetherness.

"He's not wrong," she said when she could talk again.

"Good thing I knew you guys would gang up on me like this," Jackson said, winking. "I brought enough food to feed an army."

"Yay!" Joey said and resumed jumping.

"Yay!" Stevie echoed and pretended to jump.

Jackson laughed.

"But don't make something too complicated," Stevie added. "I'm dying for that nap too."

Jackson grinned.

Christmas Day and the rest of the week passed in a merry blur. Stevie, Jackson, and Joey enjoyed time as a trio. Stevie and Jackson had couple time. And they all hung out with Marilyn and Jamie too, depending on the activity. They ate their body weights in delicious food every day. They toured the lodge's annual ice sculpture competition, and Joey was just as in awe of them as Stevie always was. This year's favorite, hands down, was a pod of killer whales. Stevie couldn't imagine how the artists even pulled it off. They went on sleigh rides and sang carols around the lodge's giant bonfire. They went tobogganing and ice-skating, accompanied by Nell and Owen one afternoon. In fact, they partook in almost every Christmassy activity on the lodge's ever-growing itinerary of festive offerings.

But the best part of the week for Stevie was all the long, much needed, far too long absent chances to talk. About serious things, yes, but also . . . just about nothing. She and Jackson talked and talked. Both of them. Not just her.

She asked Jackson more about what he'd meant about being afraid, and he shared how reading the book Marilyn loaned him triggered a memory about his mother, not something to do with his dad. How when she left, when he was even younger than Joey was now, Jackson clearly remembered wishing he hadn't made her sad so she wouldn't have left.

"Obviously, intellectually, I know I didn't make her leave. I was just a little boy—but the memory made me super uncomfortable. And then I realized I kind of feel similar when you express any kind of unhappiness. It's like I feel you're going to leave and I . . . panic. I need space. I need to protect myself."

Jackson talked very, very infrequently of his mother, and Stevie was careful to just listen. And afterward, she hugged him and told him how happy she was he'd shared that memory with her. How close it made her feel to him. It also explained, she thought, a bit of their struggles of late. They had such similar past hurts.

And they talked about Two.

"I don't want to open a second Fox & Hound to prove anything to my dad—or I don't think so. I just . . . I'm proud of what we've built. And I like the challenge."

"And I love how ambitious and passionate you are," Stevie said.

"But it's not worth it if it hurts us. We can sell it, or just . . . let it go."

"No," Stevie said. "We can make it work. And once it's off

the ground, you won't be needed there very often at all. Eloise will be a great manager."

"You're okay with her then?"

Stevie nodded. "But neither of us should cultivate close solo friendships with the opposite sex. Like she said, it's not appropriate. If you want a bestie, find a man."

"Deal."

They talked about school, and Jackson agreed that having Joey at the one closer to Fox & Hound would be way better all around.

Jackson also flashed back to Stevie's comment about wanting time to dream new dreams.

"What did you mean by that? Anything specific?"

"Actually, yeah!" Stevie shared how she thought a food truck specializing in popular street foods from around the world would go over super well in Granite Ridge and be so fun.

Jackson nodded but looked mildly disappointed.

"What?"

"Oh, nothing really. It's a great idea. I guess I wondered if maybe you were dreaming of a little Stevie Jr or something, though."

"You want another baby?"

"Maybe. Yeah—but I also love food trucks."

"I'm not opposed to a new baby. We did always say we wanted two or three—and honestly, the food truck was probably inspired by Cookie Monster."

Jackson laughed.

"And with Two, adding a food truck would be too much. But maybe I'll play with the idea for our summer menu—or we could add a food wagon to our outside patio!"

And they were off on that tangent for a bit. Just dreaming out loud for fun, not necessarily committing to anything. Riffing. But then Jackson rested his hand on Stevie's tummy.

She put her hand over his and nodded. "That's the dream we talked about that's snagged me most too."

"Right away?"

"Hmmm," she said, then winked. "As long as I can get enough rest, I don't see why not."

"Yes," Jackson agreed somberly. "A woman considering having a child does need a lot of naps." Then he pressed a slow, deep, full of dreams and promises kind of kiss on her.

And slowly, slowly as the dreamy holiday week passed, Stevie realized that the little spark of hope lit on Christmas Eve that everything would work out between them had been kindled into a blazing fire of assurance.

They had resolved this hard, hard time, not just plastered over it or ignored it and hoped things would get better. And Jackson had made a choice—to be in it, to be with her. They both loved each other. They both wanted their marriage to not merely continue, but for it to be deep and real and connected.

She was so happy—so filled with joy, actually—that when the breakdown came, it was a complete shock to her. It was their last night at the lodge, and they were snuggled up in the RV with Joey and Syd, celebrating their anniversary by eating popcorn and watching their favorite Disney classic, *The Fox and The Hound*, of course.

Joey, wiped out by his busy week of merriment, fell asleep as the credits rolled. His face was flushed, and even though he was still such a little boy, asleep, he looked even younger, remnants of his baby self still present in the soft curves of his cheeks and slightly sweaty curls. Tucked in beside him, grizzled little Syd, still in his dapper royal blue rhinestone collar, let out a snore that would make a lumberjack proud.

Jackson, who'd been studying their son too, looked up and caught Stevie's eye, his face full of love and pride. That's when it happened.

Stevie lost it. She started to cry. Or sob, more accurately.

Jackson heaved himself out of the cushions, alarm replacing his soft expression. In a flash, he had repositioned himself beside her. "What's wrong? What is it?"

"I just . . . I can't—" Stevie couldn't get the words out. Jackson put his arms around her and held her. Eventually, she calmed enough to say, "I'm sorry."

"You don't need to be sorry. What is it? Are you okay?"

She nodded against his chest, then shook her head. He shifted away slightly so that he could look her in the face.

She bit her lip. "It's just all of this." She motioned toward Jackson, then at sleeping Joey and Syd, then around at the cozy RV, aglow with Christmas lights. "This is all I've ever wanted. A family. A home. Love. It's that simple. That profound."

"Me too," Jackson said, his voice gruff.

"I know I have my sisters and moms and everybody, but I'm a woman. A mother. A wife. I want *my* family. And we almost lost it, Jackson. We—"

"Stevie . . ." Jackson sounded physically pained. He took her face in his hands and looked deeply into her eyes. What she saw reflected back was so raw, so intimate that she almost shied away, but she didn't. She held his gaze.

"You are not going to lose me, lose us, lose our family," he said. "*Ever*. And I'm so sorry that I gave you reasons to worry that you might. I will never risk the chance of you needing to ask me to leave your kitchen ever again. I promise."

Stevie shivered slightly and nodded. She was a dreamer extraordinaire, for sure. But she was also a diehard realist. How could she not be with the past she had and the things she and her loved ones had overcome and survived? She knew hard times might come again, but she chose to believe that Jackson meant his promise as much as she did hers. Because that's what you did when you loved someone. You believed them—and you believed *in* them. Besides, Stevie was also someone who knew deeply and truly that love was real. She was surrounded by it in a hundred different ways every day.

With a shuddering sigh and another nod—this one directed at her own thoughts—Stevie relaxed into Jackson's beloved embrace and let herself take comfort there.

CHAPTER 16

The hot tub was glorious, and after a day of massages, facials, hair treatments, and mani-pedis, it was a well-deserved break. Stevie definitely had a pampering-max threshold, and it had long since been reached—except for hot tubs. They were different. Hot, steamy water on an outside deck with a view of snowy mountain ranges and trees under a sky so blue it seemed like a dream? She couldn't get enough. Stevie peered through the mist at the smiling faces of those nearest and dearest to her, and a fresh surge of gratitude rushed through her. She would never not be thankful for her family. Also, they were the cutest with their pink noses and wool beanies to ward off chilly ears!

"Ah, this is lovely," Maddie said, sinking so low into the water that even her chin was submerged.

"It really, really is," Lindsey agreed.

"I'm surprised we could tear you away from *Mondo*," Stevie teased.

"And I'm surprised Stevie didn't scare him permanently away," Jo added.

Stevie waved a hand dismissively. "If he could be scared away by me or anyone, he's not good enough for Lindsey."

Lindsey laughed, but then her facial expression sobered. "In all seriousness, Stevie. I really appreciated you going all mama bear on Mondo, even though you're not my mama."

The group chuckled, and Lindsey continued, "I've never had people, *family*, to stick up for me, to be protective. It's really special, and I'm so grateful."

"I know exactly what you mean," Stevie said, looking around at her family. "We really are so blessed."

"Oh, you two," said Maddie. "You're making me all misty-eyed!"

Stevie laughed. "Like that's hard to do!"

"She has a point," said Jo, grinning. Even as kids, the sisters had always taken great glee in gently teasing Maddie about how sentimental she was—and really, it was just one more thing they all loved deeply about her. How tender she was. Especially with them.

"Still," Stevie added. "I'm glad I didn't scare him off, and I'm sorry for the misunderstanding. He seems like a great guy."

"He really, really is," Lindsey said, then went on to explain a million reasons why she thought so. It was so lovely to hear Lindsey wax on about the love she'd never expected to find that Stevie found herself unable to join in the group's banter. She was too moved.

All too soon for Stevie's liking, they were climbing out of the hot tub—but it had been mutually agreed that it was dinner time, so that was a consolation. Her stomach rumbled at the very thought of food as if cheering in agreement.

There were squeals and shrieks as their warm bodies hit the frigid air and their pruney feet touched down on the frosty deck. When they were all dried off and dressed again, they headed out of the lodge in search of eats to please the whole group. They didn't have to go far. Kitty-corner from the lodge's main entrance, classic rock piped into the night air from a pub with a sleek aluminum marquee that read The Bar. Golden light shone onto the snow from its slightly steamy mullioned windows. Stevie knew it well, of course. It was Jackson's old pub, formerly known as Jackson's Public House.

"Oh, let's eat here!" Maddie said. "We can see if the food is as tasty as Jackson's was."

"It's not," Stevie said loyally—and not lying. "But it is really good."

"That settles it! If it even remotely has your stamp of approval, we're in," Lindsey said, opening the glass door with a flourish.

Stevie and Jackson always made a point of eating at The Bar for old times' sake, but that didn't keep her heart from lurching as they stepped into the steamy warmth of the crowded pub. The new owners hadn't redecorated, and who could blame them? From the cheery, booze-fueled laughter and chatter of customers to the mingled aromas of deep-fried treats and roasting meat to the clanking of cutlery and rush of servers with trays of drinks and food, it was perfect. And such a place of happy memories for her.

It was just as busy as it had been under Jackson's owner-ship, but they were lucky. A large group was just settling their tab and vacating a table.

They agreed on a whole bunch of appetizers to share instead of meals, and once their server had taken their drinks and food order, Maddie turned to Stevie, eyes warm. "Is it fun to see your reunion spot again, or is it bitter-sweet?"

"It's surprisingly touching every time I visit, actually," Stevie admitted.

"Does six years feel like a long time?"

"Like forever and also like a blink."

"Yes," Jo said. "That sums up so many relationship things, doesn't it?"

"Especially raising kids," Maddie said, giving Jo and Stevie fond looks. "For me, it feels like just yesterday that the four of you arrived in my house and took over my heart, and now here you are . . . women with kids, not even just babies. *Kids.*"

At the words *four of you*, Stevie's heart panged a little. "I wish Alissa and Hailey could've been here."

"Well . . . " Maddie raised her glass and beamed. "Good news on that front! No promises, of course, but they each made comments during our Christmas calls that sounded a whole lot like they're planning to be here next year."

"Omigoodness!" Jo's excited tone suggested she'd already discounted Maddie's "no promises" and had moved into planning mode. Her next words confirmed it. "We should book rooms here at the lodge now, just in case!"

"Oh, yes," Maddie agreed. "A Cedar Mountain Lodge Christmas with everybody together again would be magical."

There were a few minutes of happy buzz about the idea, and then their drinks arrived, distracting them. Maddie took a long, appreciative sip of the red wine she'd ordered and turned to Stevie once more.

"It's such a relief to see you at peace and happy again," she said simply. "You and Jackson are good then? You've worked out whatever it was?"

Startled, Stevie put down her mug of mulled apple cider.

"Oh, don't look so shocked," Maddie said. "I've been your mother for how long? I know when something's not right with you."

"Yeah," Stevie said. "Things are . . . good. Really good, in fact."

Maddie's eyes were soft. "I'm so glad."

Stevie felt stupidly on the verge of crying. "I'm sorry I didn't tell you. I didn't mention anything to Marilyn either, though Jackson kind of gave it away to her—" She broke off talking. All these extraneous details weren't the meat and potatoes of what she wanted to say. "I didn't want to worry you until I knew for sure if there was something to be worried about, and I didn't want to color anyone against Jackson by accident if everything ended up being fine."

"That's very wise, strong, and generous—in other words, totally *you*."

Stevie shook her head but smiled, feeling just as thrilled and loved by Maddie's way of seeing her as she had as an angry, confused thirteen-year-old kid all those years ago.

"I hope you know that you can always come to me with anything, though, right? Just like you could then, you can now."

"I do know that. For sure. Thank you."

Maddie nodded, her smile saying a million kind things. Stevie hoped her eyes would always transmit the love for her family that Maddie's did for hers.

Jo let out a whooshing sigh. "You already know how relieved and happy I am about your news, Stevie."

Stevie did. They'd had a long talk after she and Jackson returned from their Cedar Mountain Lodge escapade.

"But yeesh," Jo continued. "Life is really hard sometimes, isn't it?"

"Yeah," Stevie agreed. "But even the hardest bits are survivable when a person has loved ones like you guys."

"Aw, hear, hear," Lindsey said, lifting her wineglass. "And may it ever be so."

Raising her glass to toast along with the others, part of Stevie wondered when she'd become such a sentimental cheeseball—and another part of her knew that she'd always had this soft side. Just now, all these years into her life, it was finally safe for her to just be . . . her. All facets of herself. She was tough. She was a survivor. She was also . . . vulnerable and just wanted the people she loved to be safe and happy. And for them to love her and hold her close in thought and deed. And right now, they all were. And they did. She decided to adopt Lindsey's lovely words too. *May it ever be so.*

The server arrived with a huge tray bearing all sorts of delectable tidbits. Stevie dug into the food with her family, knowing that soon her stomach would be just as full as her heart. So practically bursting.

EPILOGUE

Jo and Luke's house, the one Stevie and the rest of the Soul Sisters had first become a family in so many, many years ago now, was practically bursting at the seams. The whole family—all her sisters, their husbands, their kids, and their kids' families, plus her own brood, and Maddie and Robert, Lindsey and Armando, and Marilyn and Jamie—had gathered for Christmas this year.

The chaos and noise were all part of the fun, though, and Stevie reveled in it, even if her ears needed a break. She'd been up since five a.m. getting food ready for the crowd. Now, with dinner over and games starting in various corners of the house and as cousins and grandkids pulled out card tables and set up a ping pong table downstairs, she decided to slip out to the verandah and catch a few minutes alone.

As she tried to sneak out unseen, Marilyn, Maddie, and her Aunt Lindsey, whose pretty silver-haired heads were bent in close conversation, all turned toward her as if sensing she was trying to escape.

"Busted," Stevie said, laughing. "I just need to catch a moment of quiet. Don't tell the kids."

"Your secret's safe with us," Maddie said.

"You could say mums the word," Marilyn added with a wink, and Stevie groaned at the terrible pun.

"Take all the time you need," Maddie said.

"Dinner was superb," Marilyn added. "You outdid yourself yet again."

Stevie just smiled. Marilyn still said that *every* year.

"Scoot before someone needs you!" encouraged Lindsey.

The cold night air was delicious on Stevie's flushed face. This menopause stuff was for the birds! But her light inner complaining was cut short as she caught sight of the star-studded velvet sky.

Jo and Luke kept a big wicker rocking chair on the porch, just the way Maddie always had. The porch swing was still there too.

Stevie settled herself into the chair and was suddenly hit with deja vu so strong it was like the past 42 years had fallen away, and she along with them. She was thirteen years old again. She'd snuck out that first Christmas too, just to think and feel . . . needing to process all the mixed emotions she'd had then. Hope, joy, grief, longing . . . Tonight, though, there was only joy and gratitude. If only she could go back to her lonely kid self and tell her of the miracles to come. The family—the huge, huge extended family—she would end up having! And what would've surprised kid Stevie even more—that she'd have two children of her own, at least one grand-baby, and, from the way life was looking, quite possibly more. It was crazy: something both younger Stevie and her current self could agree on.

"It all works out, punk kid," she whispered. "Better than you can even imagine."

The door to the porch burst open, and noisy voices and laughter poured into the night air, then just as quickly were stifled as the door shut again. Stevie turned. "Oh, it's you."

"Disappointed?"

"Hmm," she said, shrugging as a joke, then spoke the truth. "Never ever."

She squeezed over to one side of the wide chair and patted the empty space beside her. "Sit cozy?"

"Mmmm, yes, please."

Stevie shook her head, smiling.

Jackson settled in beside her, then nestled her close under his arm. She breathed in his figs and lime scent. Thank goodness her hot flash had faded. His closeness in the weather that her body was finally registering as dead of winter was delicious. He grinned down at her like he was reading her thoughts, causing a new and not unwelcome one to simmer. That had been such a happy surprise for her—that their love would only get hotter over the years, and it had been wonderfully spicy from the get-go. Not that there hadn't been ups and downs, of course. You couldn't live a long life and not have some struggles and difficult times. But as they both loved to say to make their children groan, they paired well together. *May it ever be so*, Stevie thought.

The door banged again.

"Mom! There you are!"

Stevie grinned up at her tall, red-headed daughter. For all the world, Julia sounded like Stevie had fled the country or something.

"Can you hold Stevie? Ivy and Joe pawned her off on me, and I think she wants to sleep, but it's so loud in there—and I want to play Twister."

Stevie and Jackson both laughed at that. Julia had loved that game since she was a toddler, playing it with her much older brother and cousins.

"Of course!" Stevie said, reaching out. "I can never get enough of her, you know that!"

Stevie took her tiny namesake, who was wrapped like a

burrito in an adorable flannel blanket that had pink cupcakes all over it. Pressing a kiss to her granddaughter's sweet little head—a head covered with downy fox-red hair—she marveled aloud. "Imagine us having a married twenty-seven-year-old son with a baby and a twenty-one-year-old daughter."

"Who, from the sounds of it, definitely *doesn't* have baby fever."

"Or not yet anyway," Stevie said, laughing. She happened to know there was a boy back in Uni that Julia talked about a lot—and who said he wanted six kids. She'd let that be a surprise for Jackson.

Jackson reached out and traced little Stevie's peach-like cheek. "She is some kind of precious, isn't she?"

"Yes," Stevie agreed. It had come as a shock to her—how deeply, instantly, and utterly profoundly she loved this little girl. She hadn't known it would be just as intense as the love she'd felt for her own children. The human heart was such an amazing thing. How love just made room for more love.

Jackson's arm around her shoulder tightened.

"What?" she asked, looking up at him.

His beautiful dark eyes were shiny with emotion—or maybe it was just the glow of the Christmas lights framing the porch.

"I'm just so grateful, Fox."

Nope, she'd been right the first time. Emotion. "Me too," she whispered. "Me too."

Together, they watched the sky and admired baby Stevie. Eventually, when it grew too cold for even perpetually-hot-these-days Stevie to bear it, they got up to go in.

Hand on the door, just about to open it for her and baby Stevie, Jackson paused. "I was thinking of booking us a week, just the two of us, at Cedar Mountain Lodge. What do you think?"

"That it sounds absolutely perfect."

Jackson beamed and motioned for her to go first, but Stevie paused for a second on the threshold, treasuring the noise and love evident in every shriek and laugh, ready to rejoin the party.

As she had observed so many times over the years, she was beyond lucky. Her blessings had surpassed all her dreams. So many, many times over.

Dear Reader,

Thank you so much for reading *Christmas Comfort*. I hope you enjoyed it and that you love Stevie and her family as much as I do. The minute the word comfort came to me, I knew it was the title for this story because writing it brought me a lot of comfort, personally.

Stevie resonated with me deeply from the very first time she stalked into my head, hoodie pulled up, hiding her face, fists clenched and buried deep in her pockets: proud and angry, shy and insecure, deeply sad yet holding tight to dreams—even while certain none of those dreams could come true for her.

And don't we all feel like that at various times in our lives? Damaged by people who should have loved us best. Rejected. Terrified. Angry. Desperately sad. Hopefully, like Stevie, we find our true people, and over time, healing comes to us and to those we love as well.

I am so fortunate to have a huge extended family—family related by blood and by heart—just like Stevie. And I see each of my novels in this series almost as thank-you letters or love notes to my family, who encourage me and lift me up every day. Life, as Jo observes during their conversation at the spa, is really hard sometimes—and yet, as Stevie notes (in slightly different words!), even the hardest bits are survivable when you've got loved ones you can depend on.

I hope you, dear reader, have the kinds of friends and family who love you to your bones and walk beside you through all your times, the good, the bad, and everything in between. May it be so!

Much love to you, and huge thanks for reading,

Ev

ALSO BY EV BISHOP

STANDALONES

Bigger Things

A Sharla Brown Christmas

SAIL AWAY SERIES

A Not So Distant Shore

RIVER'S SIGH B & B

Wedding Bands (Book 1)

Hooked (Book 2)

Spoons (Book 3)

Hook, Line & Sinker (Book 4)

Silver Bells (Book 5) *Reeling* (Book 6)

New Year's Resolution: One to Keep (Book 7)

The Catch (Book 8) *River's Sigh B & B Vol. 1 – 4*

River's Sigh B & B Vol. 5 – 8

THE SECOND CHANCE SHOP

Something Old (Book 1)

Something New (Book 2)

SOUL SISTERS AT CEDAR MOUNTAIN LODGE

Christmas Sisters – prologue book

Christmas Kisses by Judith Keim

Christmas Wishes by Tammy L. Grace

Christmas Hope by Violet Howe

Christmas Dreams by Ev Bishop

Christmas Rings by Tess Thompson

Christmas Surprises by Tammy L. Grace

Christmas Yearnings by Ev Bishop

Christmas Peace by Violet Howe

Christmas Castles by Judy Keim

Christmas Star by Tess Thompson

Christmas Joy by Judith Keim

Christmas Shelter by Tammy L. Grace

Christmas Secret by Violet Howe

Christmas Longings by Ev Bishop

Christmas Promise by Violet Howe

Christmas Comfort by Ev Bishop

Christmas Hearts by Tammy L. Grace

Visit www.evbishop.com for information about upcoming works, to sign up for *Ev's News*, or to drop her a line. She'd love to hear from you!

ABOUT EV BISHOP

Ev Bishop is an award-winning, *USA Today* bestselling author, best known for her small-town contemporary romance series, River's Sigh B & B. Readers describe her books as "full of humor, love and wisdom," set in places "where breathtaking scenery and the magic of love are the best medicine for the soul."

When Ev's nose isn't in a book or her fingers aren't on her keyboard, you'll find her with her family and dogs or playing outside, usually at the lake or in an overgrown garden somewhere.

She loves any and all garden related talk and work, cooking (and eating!), and making all sorts of random things, especially out of upcycled or reclaimed items.